Of Trolls

And

Evil Things

Of Trolls and Evil Things

Of Trolls and Evil Things by Richard H. Stephens

http://www.richardhstephens.com/

Cover by Marco Pennacchietti

Hardcover ISBN: 978-1-775-1036-5-3

Of Trolls and Evil Things

Other books by Richard H. Stephens

***The Royal Tournament* (78 pg. novella)**

The Royal Tournament has at long last come to the sleepy village of Millsford. For Javen Milford, a local farm boy, the news couldn't be better. Finally, Javen can perform his chores on the homestead and partake in the biggest military games in the kingdom, hoping beyond hope, that just maybe, he might catch the eye of the king.

Javen's expertise in jousting holds him in good stead running the tilts in the tournament's flagship event. The local supporters believe Javen is more than ready to step up to the challenge and defeat the tournament's reigning *Emperor of the Field*, Prince Malcolm.

Unfortunately for naive Javen, he befriends a mystical foreign entrant and quickly learns how ruthless men can be. It doesn't take long for him to realize that the biggest challenge facing him is not whether to duck or parry, but whether to confront his newest revelations and take the chance that will have him fighting for his very life.

Now available on Amazon for e-book and paperback, and at Lulu.com for hardcover.

Soul Forge (500 pg. Epic Fantasy)

Scorned by an ungrateful kingdom, unfairly blaming him for the demise of their beloved Queen, Silurian Mintaka decides he can't fight for his kingdom anymore. To re-enter the hostile fray of his peers would probably end up with him killing them all.

An old man reaches through his darkness, convincing him the people's need outweighs his loathing of them. Befriending a few eccentric characters along the way, Silurian Mintaka faces a whirlwind of drastic choices, that once made, may lead to the deaths of those he is entrusted to protect.

Embarking upon the greatest journey of their lives, they travel the uncharted waters of the Niad Ocean. Not across, but beneath, on a fool's errand to recover the lost enchantment of his fabled blade.

Available at the beginning of 2018

Wizard of the North (Book 2 of the *Soul Forge* trilogy)

Available late spring, 2018

Of Trolls and Evil Things

Of Trolls and Evil Things

Now that the first book is published, the journey is still a very exciting one to undertake, but it has proven a lot less daunting. That being said, it would never have been completed without the incredible support and feedback of my Beta readers. Thank you, Caroline Davidson, Jordan Brown, Joshua Stephens, Louise Spilsbury, Matthew Lane and Paul Stephens. Without you, this book would have never left the draft stage.

Again, I find myself in awe of the man who creates my beautiful cover art, Marco Pennacchietti. Thank you for giving my characters a face. You can check out his amazing artwork at: https://www.artstation.com/deimos23390

You can also contact him directly at:
pennacchietti23marco@gmail.com

This book is dedicated to my Mom and Dad. Thank you for the love and invaluable life lessons you taught me along the way. Though I may not have seemed to be listening at the time, they have made me the person I am today, and for that, I am grateful. Until we meet again.

Of Trolls and Evil Things

Of Trolls

And

Evil Things

Of Trolls and Evil Things

Table of Contents

Hairy's Haunt

"**Mel.** Wake up, we gotta go." Silurian, a dirty faced, teenaged boy, bent low in a dark cave, attempting to awaken his sister asleep upon the ground. Locating her shoulder, he grabbed it and shook hard. "Come on, we gotta go now!"

The girl sat bolt upright, scaring him half to death. She took a moment to gather her wits before asking with a squeak, "The troll?"

"Yes, our friend, Hairy. If we don't get out of here fast, we're going to become his breakfast."

The girl jumped to her feet and followed her brother from the cave; the entrance evidenced by a faint light permeating the dank surroundings. The troll's heavy breathing followed them as it chased them from deeper within the catacombs of Mount Cinder.

Bursting from the cave, they were blinded by the early morning sun. They ran a hundred yards across the mountain face and fell into a heap amongst a patch of tall grass.

Lying on his stomach, breathing hard, Silurian parted the tall grass and scanned the cave mouth, barely visible from this distance. His ice blue eyes surveyed the scene. His long, black hair fluttered about his face in the cool breeze wafting up the mountainside, a faint scent of salt water accompanying the sporadic gusts. Gleaning with sweat, he panted, "Don't worry. He won't…venture…into the sunlight. Trolls abhor any kind of light."

Melody sat beside her brother, eyes wide with fear. A thick mane of golden hair fell past her shoulder blades, buffeted by the wind. She absently pushed aside the fine wisps from her face, unconvinced the troll would be put off by the sunshine basking the mountainside. Sniffing at the air with her button nose, she too, could smell the brine in the air.

Though not sheer, the mountainside dropped away at a dizzying angle toward unseen depths below, plunging into the Unknown Sea, an expanse of water turbulently abutting the entire northern shore of Zephyr. All along the mountain face, pine trees clutched for life amidst jumbles of large boulders.

Melody's gaze travelled to the misted heights, pondering what dangerous animals might call the summit home. Perhaps she and Silurian would be better off finding a cave up there. Surely the troll that had been hounding them for the past few weeks wouldn't track them above the snowline.

Snowline. She almost laughed out loud. Her gaze drifted to her brother's ripped and worn leather leggings; threadbare, and gaping at the knees. They would freeze to death long before the mountain denizens were even aware of their presence.

She spotted a tear in his tattered leather shirt, behind his left shoulder. A wet, dark crimson stain surrounded the odd-looking rip. She leaned in to inspect it.

"What happened to your shoulder?"

He shrugged her concern away, his mind elsewhere, thinking about the events earlier in the morning that led them to this point.

"Did Hairy do that?"

"No Mel, I had an itch," Silurian said, pulling away from her fussing.

Seeing her crestfallen face, he gave her a half smile, and told her what had happened.

He had awoken a little while ago, just before the sunrise. Lying in the dark cave, he had tried to go back to sleep, but the sound of water dripping close by, beckoned him, he was so thirsty. He had had misgivings about leaving her alone, but he didn't intend on wandering far. If he couldn't find the source within a few minutes, he planned to return to her side and wait for morning.

Of Trolls and Evil Things

Using a chipped flint stone and crude hunting knife, he lit a brand and ventured into the deeper mountain byways that led from the rear of the cave.

Flickering flames enveloped him within a cocoon of light, the oppressive darkness beyond, absolute.

The tunnel walls, dry for the most part, served as subterranean lava vents. The ceiling dipped low in places, causing him to duck his head.

Before venturing far, he stopped up short, sensing a presence between himself and his sleeping sister.

Prickly tendrils of fear washed over him.

The troll.

He didn't know how he knew the troll was there, hidden within an unseen crevice he had already passed, but know he did. Fighting to quell the fear rooting him to the ground, he sniffed at the air, cursing himself for not having noticed the odour before.

They had slept along the face of Mount Cinder over the past few weeks, opting to brave the perils of the numerous caves dotting the mountainside. Even with the occasional run-in with the troll, and Silurian was certain it was the same troll every time, they believed sleeping in a cave a lesser evil to camping under the stars at the mercy of the mountain's nocturnal predators.

The smell dissipated. The troll was moving away from him. Toward his sister.

Sprinting back the way he had come, the makeshift torch's meager light flitted uselessly around him. As a result, he careened off the twisting tunnel walls. Fumbling for his crude hunting knife, he frantically attempted to intercept the troll before it reached Melody.

Without thinking, he yelled for his sister to wake up.

The odour in the dark corridor became stronger, and he ran straight into the matted, hairy chest of their stalker.

In the fire's light, the troll's beady, yellow eyes were wet and raw. Its flat snout, dripping mucous, sat crookedly above yellowed teeth coated with vestiges of a recent meal.

The beast snarled, shunning the light.

The search for his knife forgotten, Silurian instinctively threw his arms over his head to protect himself, causing the torch to accidentally brush the troll's face.

The troll howled in pain, thrashing its arms in a frenzied attempt to strike away the offending brand. One of its forearms connected with Silurian's hand and he lost his grip on it.

The torch whirled through the air. Banging off a wall, sparks flew in all directions as it bounced farther down the passageway, leaving the combatants in wavering shadows.

The troll lashed out, trying to connect with the animal that had caused it pain. It felt its claws rip into flesh. Lunging toward the ensuing yelp of pain, it missed the boy, and staggered. Before regaining its balance, a vicious blow impacted the side of its left knee, collapsing it to the granite floor in agony.

The weight of the troll toppled over Silurian, but he was able to roll free, and got quickly back to his feet.

If nothing else, his experience with this troll over the past few weeks taught him that the beast could see quite well in the dark. He hazarded a longing glance down the passage, beyond the writhing troll, to the sputtering torch on the floor. If he went back for it, he would lose the precious little time he had gained by felling the beast. It would also put him on its wrong side.

He scrambled up the passageway, away from the troll and the dying brand, and ran full tilt into a rock wall. Stunned, he shook his head and staggered backward, struggling to remain upright. Finding his bearings, he groped his way through the darkness. He had to reach his sister before the troll reached him.

The cool morning air outside the cave eased aside as a warm front crept up the mountainside. Puffy, white clouds lolled aimlessly above the two teenaged children huddled together upon Mount Cinder.

Melody inspected her brother's shoulder. She helped him take off his shirt, wincing every time he did. Together they had found the plants required to make a poultice, and she attempted to secure the leaf-wrapped concoction to his weeping sore.

"It looks infected," she said, her lips close to his ear as she worked.

"Of course it's infected. A troll did it."

Melody ignored his patronizing tone. "I think you should get it looked at in town. Besides, I'm hungry. We haven't eaten anything but roots and leaves for a week."

"Okay," Silurian muttered. His pinched brow softened seeing her melancholy face. "Okay."

Melody carefully helped him into his shirt, and stared out across the white capped stretches of the Unknown Sea.

Silurian shrugged, testing the poultice's ability to remain in place. Satisfied, he wondered what his sister was thinking. He had snapped at her when all she was trying to do was care for him. She didn't deserve that. He followed her gaze toward the horizon, marvelling at how much she resembled their mother.

Their mother. How he missed her. How, he knew, Melody missed her. He placed a hand upon her outstretched thigh. "I'm sorry I snapped at you. You know I meant you no harm."

Melody pushed away a stray lock of hair from her eyes. She covered his hand with her own, gazing into his ice blue eyes. "I know you didn't. You're as hungry as I am. Probably more."

She became quiet once more, staring out to sea, trying to marshal the nerve to broach a touchy subject. Inhaling deeply, she said in a quick breath, "I want to go with you."

Silurian's head whipped about. "What? You know you can't come with me. We've been over this a hundred times. It's not safe for you to wander the streets of Cliff Face. It's not even safe for *me* to be seen hanging around there too long. If the vagrants catch me, they take everything I earn. If they take an interest in me, well, I'd rather not think about what they would do. Do you forget what these people wanted to do to you? Think hard, because I've seen what they do to girls who fall within their shadow." Silurian let his gaze drop to the ground, trying to ignore the dark memories. He whispered, “It’s not nice.”

She had known what his response would be before she suggested it. She was aware of the evils awaiting an orphan girl caught roaming the streets with no one to protect her, but a month of hiding in the mountains weighed upon her. They hid in the wilderness to protect her, not him. She knew that he sacrificed the chance of a better life for her sake. He put up with the cold, the hunger and the constant threat of the troll, for her, and she loved him dearly for it. She also knew autumn fast approached. They would be hard put to survive the winter up here.

She had suggested a while ago that they hit the trail. Journey to Castle Svelte, the royal house of Zephyr, hundreds of leagues to the south. Throw themselves upon the mercy of the court. Surely, a noble king wouldn’t forsake their plight.

Silurian had forbidden it. He said he refused to burden anyone else with their problems. Not if he could help it. If they wished to succeed, they must do it on their own. He was as stubborn as their father.

She smiled, despite her mood. At fourteen, she was also becoming a young adult. With as much consternation as she could muster, she said, “I’m afraid, Sil. What if the troll comes for me when you go into Cliff Face? What if animals wander down from the heights in search of food? What if—”

Silurian got to his feet. “What if this. What if that. What if those nasty men in Cliff Face take a shine to you? I can’t protect you. You know that. Dad made me promise not to let anything happen to you. He knew we would be in for a tough time. He knew the people we would have to deal with.”

Dark clouds massed far out to sea, drifting toward them from over the horizon. He said to the wind more than to her, “And I aim to keep that promise.”

They didn’t speak for a while. The wind blew in colder. The ominous clouds continued to coalesce over the choppy waters. They were in for a bad one.

He sighed. His sister rested her forehead upon forearms draped across raised knees. He wanted to say something else, but thought better of it.

On the wind came the scent of rain. Remaining exposed upon the mountain, defying the oncoming storm, wasn't a great idea.

"Alright," he said softly, the words snatched away by the wind. He cleared his throat. "Alright, Mel. You win. You can come to town with me today," he finished almost inaudibly.

Melody's breath caught in her throat. Jumping to her feet and clasping her hands together as if in prayer, she hopped with joy.

"Really? Really?" She bounced around in a circle. "I can't believe it. I'm going to town. Oh, I'm so excited." She hopped over to her brother who regarded her with mimicked boredom. She threw her arms around him, holding him tight. Hopping about again, she forced him to the balls of his feet and had him reeling to catch his balance.

She squealed, "Thank you, thank you, thank you."

"Alright. Alright. Alright!" He broke her grip and backed away a step. "Don't get too excited. You're not going to like what I have to say next."

Her bouncing stopped.

He scanned the horizon, the black wall of clouds already halfway across the sea toward them. The storm would be on them before the hour. If they had any chance of finding shelter in Cliff Face before it hit, they needed to get off the mountain now.

"We have to cut your hair," he said matter-of-factly.

Melody looked at him as if he had just sprouted horns.

"I mean *cut* your hair."

He wasn't talking about a trim.

"Oh, no. You can't." She grabbed at the lengths of hair behind her neck, horrified. "You're not serious, are you? Tell me you're kidding."

Silurian stood before her and sighed.

"You are serious," she gasped. "But why, Sil, why?"

"Come on. We both know what happens if you go to Cliff Face looking like a girl. You barely escaped last time. I can't protect you against armed men. Heck, I can't protect you against unarmed men."

"But my hair? It's the only nice thing I have left," she pleaded. "Why can't I just tuck it inside my tunic?" She proceeded to do so. "See? No more hair."

Silurian frowned. He raised his right hand, motioning for her to twirl around.

Melody spun about quickly, holding her breath. A sizable bulge protruded at the nape of her neck where her hair disappeared beneath the fabric.

He dropped his forehead into an upturned palm.

Her shoulders slumped, her hopeful smile slipping from her face. Stamping her feet, she walked toward the cave, pulling her hair free.

"Where are you going?"

Her receding backside was the only reply he received. He glanced at the approaching storm. If they ran all the way, they might escape the worst of it.

"Mel!" Silurian raced after her. "Mel, wait up."

She stopped, crossing her arms over her chest, but wouldn't turn around.

He came up behind her, placing a hand on her shoulder.

She shrugged it off. Turning, she glared, tears rolling off her cheeks. "What?"

"Where are you going? Can't you see the storm almost upon us?"

As if on cue, a cold, briny wind tossed their hair about.

Melody shifted her stance, her gaze boring into his. "Of course I can see the storm. I'm not stupid, you know. I'm going back to the cave."

"The cave?" he blurted. "You can't go back to the cave. Are you insane? Our friend Hairy is probably watching us right now, for heaven's sake."

"And just what do you expect me to do? Sit out here and enjoy the weather?" She sniffed, raising a single eyebrow in scorn; a facial mannerism passed down from their mother. "For heaven's sake."

"Aw, come on, Mel." His thoughts raced. There wasn't another cave that he knew of for at least a league in any direction. There was no way she should have to weather the elements, especially alone. Doing so on the face of Mount Cinder would be more dangerous than risking the troll. There was nothing to do but take her with him.

"Come on. If we run, we might beat the storm."

"I'm not cutting my hair."

"Fine, let's just go."

He began jogging toward the distant city of Cliff Face, unseen around the bulk of Mount Cinder. As he ran, he felt the light pressure of the poultice beneath his tunic. He glanced over his left shoulder at the tear in his dirty shirt, grimacing at the darkened area and the blood he had spent. *It'll heal*, he thought.

He was relieved Melody remained close behind, the sound of her footfalls lost in the whistling wind. Her long, flaxen hair blew about behind her. Shaking his head, he kept running.

While they navigated a faint path, Silurian's mind wandered. Listening to his own laboured breathing, he recalled the night their parents were murdered. His eyes misted. He couldn't shake the nightmarish images from his mind. Nor a few of the encounters they had experienced since then…

Thief

Silurian remembered the day he fled with his sister from the chaotic scene unfolding outside their peaceful homestead. A month ago, a band of armed men had descended upon their farm for no reason that made sense to him.

His father had exclaimed to their mother, "Mase, find the children quick! They've found us!"

Silurian could still see the alarm on his father's face as he ushered them out the back door. With no time to offer an explanation, their father's desperate plea chased them into the hills, "Silurian, remember, you must protect your sister at all costs. Now run!"

They spent that first night on Mount Cinder hidden beneath the low boughs of a large pine tree, too terrified to go home, but equally afraid of being caught upon the slopes after dark. Neither one slept.

Early the following morning, weariness and hunger began to take their toll, sapping their strength and doubling them over in pain. Not knowing what to do, Silurian decided they should head toward Cliff Face in search of help.

Inside the city walls they found themselves with no place to go. No one would listen to their strange story. The guards at the city gate wouldn't even give them the time of day.

Afraid to return home, they were forced to start begging for food, but the citizens of Cliff Face, all too familiar with beggars, paid them little mind. Rougher individuals pushed them to the ground, advising them to be on their way lest they find out what happens to vagrants who bother decent folk.

They managed to scrounge a few rotten fruits for their efforts that first day in Cliff Face before the sun fell behind Mount Cinder. With the shadows lengthening toward dusk, the atmosphere in the city changed. Gone were the merchants and peddlers hawking their wares. In their wake, ruffians of all descriptions spilled into the streets, reeking of ale and smoke. Barely dressed women hung off their burly arms, their language so colourful, Silurian's ears turned red.

Melody's mouth hung open in disbelief. Women were thrown to the street while the perpetrator stood over them, shouting abuse. Other women had their clothes ripped from their shoulders, but instead of crying out, they laughed and held the man responsible, closer. Nor was this type of behaviour limited to the men. There were many tough looking women unloading tirades of expletives on cowering males.

A fight broke out inside a tavern and spilled into the street, the combatants followed outside by the irate proprietor brandishing a meat cleaver and ringing a well-used bell over his head; the clapper pealing an annoying cadence to summon the City Watch.

Melody's presence drew the attention of the seedier characters, who directed crude remarks her way. A naïve, country girl, she knew enough to realize she didn't want to find out what they meant by, 'having a good time,' or letting someone, 'be her pappy.'

She clung to Silurian as they backed down the street, but they weren't quick enough. Half a dozen men came up from behind, surrounding them. Belching men with foul breath, offered them mischievous, tooth missing grins. One man went as far as patting Melody's bottom, laughing in delight at the sport.

She screamed.

Silurian kicked him in the shin.

The man's grin disappeared. Spitting, he produced a large knife and stepped in front of Silurian. An evil sneer twisted his bearded face.

Silurian retreated in fear, but his escape was cut short as he backed into another large man who grabbed him by the neck and thrust him forward. Silurian staggered to a quick stop inches from the knifepoint waggling beneath his chin.

A horn blew from somewhere close by. The man with the knife withdrew the blade and scrambled away, following the rest of those gathered, down side alleyways. Twenty mounted knights charged up the street toward the bell ringer, not giving the teenaged children a second glance.

Silurian cared less whether the Watch took an interest in them or not. Their arrival had served to rescue his sister and himself from an unsavoury fate. He took the opportunity to lead her out of harm's way and headed for the city gate.

The sentries at the gate refused to lift the heavy portcullis at such a late hour, but Silurian felt safer close to the defended barbican.

Though the guards wouldn't dare harm a girl while on duty, they kept a furtive eye on Melody. If she concentrated hard enough she could catch snatches of their snickering conversation. Her cheeks turned bright red.

Come morning, two days after their farm had been sacked, they slipped down Redfire Path and made the half day journey back to the homestead.

Any hope they had of their parents surviving the raid was dashed as they rounded a bend in the path overlooking their home in a glen far below. Tendrils of black smoke wisped from two large piles of charred wood where their home and barn had once stood.

On closer inspection, they were almost relieved to find two fresh graves dug beneath the big oak tree they used to climb in the back yard. Somebody, perhaps a neighbour from one of the distant farms, had come by and saw to the burial. At least they didn't have to witness what those butchers had done to their mother and father.

The graves were simply marked with two sticks each, one stick bound crosswise with twine near the top of a longer one that marked the head of each plot. The cross on the left grave had already tipped to one side.

Of Trolls and Evil Things

Jogging along the windy mountainside, traces of rain stung their eyes. They were still at least an hour away from Cliff Face. Silurian could hear Melody huffing and puffing behind him. Making sure his sister didn't see the pain in his eyes as the memories of what happened to their parents assaulted him, he made a conscious effort to turn his thoughts to a trip he had taken to Cliff Face on his own a few weeks ago…

They had decided that it was much safer for both of them if Melody remained away from the city and the evil things that were wont to happen within its walls, so Silurian took it upon himself to venture into the city every couple of days in an effort to earn them something decent to eat.

He had had no luck finding work this particular day. Sitting despondent upon a merchant's front step, he ignored his grumbling stomach and pondered what to do.

The rotund, balding, store owner came outside wearing a dirty apron, demanding he go haunt some other shop. Silurian got up to leave, then decided to take a chance and asked the merchant if he had any tasks needing done in return for a scrap or two. Maybe even a copper.

The merchant considered him. "Hmmm? Now that you mention it, I do have a rather large load of provisions I need hauled into the back. Not sure about a copper, but I'm sure I can fix you up something to eat. If you're quick, I may even use you again, huh?"

Silurian nodded eagerly.

"Wait here. I'll get you set up in a few minutes." The man entered his shop, stopping to hold the door open for a middle-aged couple that were creaking up the front porch steps.

Smiling at his good fortune, Silurian watched as an older woman beneath a ratty, straw hat, exited the shop and made her way between the middle-aged couple. The small sack she carried brushed against the woman, twisting it in her hand. An apple and an onion popped free, dropping to the dirt street with nary a sound. Silurian snatched up the produce and went to hand them back, but the old lady hadn't missed a step. She had already joined the throng in the street.

He stared at his prize, so hungry it hurt. The receding woman's backside limped away, losing herself in the bustle of the marketplace. He shined the apple on his tunic. If he ate half the apple now, he could save the other half for Mel.

He could just make out the woman's tattered hat bobbing along. With a huge sigh, he got to his feet and scampered after her. After all, they weren't his.

Catching up to the old lady, Silurian had spent the next little while listening to her go on about a great many things that he had no idea of what she was talking about. It would be rude to walk away, especially from an elder, so he listened politely and nodded when it seemed the proper time to do so, though all he could think about was getting back to the merchant. A simple thank you would have been more than sufficient.

When he returned to the mercantile a short while later he was told the position had been filled in his absence. Nor was he to show his face around there again.

Dejected, he decided the more affluent marketplace wasn't panning out, so he took to plying his trade amongst the seedier merchants peddling their goods in the lower part of the city.

His clothing and appearance didn't warrant a second glance in the western marketplace. He was as well-kempt as any of the belching vendors.

He managed to land a backbreaking chore lugging heavy crates from a wagon into the rear of a shop, only to be tossed onto the road by the scruff of his neck in lieu of payment. When the man responsible for his harsh treatment glared at him with arms crossed, Silurian could only smile, get to his feet, and set off down the street in hopes of securing a more lucrative job somewhere else. It wasn't the first time he had been treated so poorly.

Tired, sore and hungry, he sat down beside a farmer's cart laden with delicious looking produce. A large farmer stood between the cart and a ramshackle, wooden table he used to prepare his customer's orders.

Silurian hung his head between his knees in despair, his arms slumped between his legs. He had no idea how long he sat there like that, but the squeak of a young girl's voice broke through his melancholy.

A grimy-faced girl, clad in a simple, tattered, brown shift, cinched about her tiny waist with a frayed length of filthy twine, stood before the farmer's table. She couldn't have been much older than ten.

Silurian smiled at the cute face hidden behind a mask of dirt as she shyly placed her order.

The farmer gave her a once over and shot her a skeptical look.

The girl produced a tiny burlap pouch bound by another piece of twine. Plunking it proudly upon the table, her face beaming, she proclaimed, "I have money."

The farmer grunted and turned to his cart to assemble her order.

While the farmer's back was to the table, a huge man approached. He bumped into the girl, almost knocking her to the ground. The girl shrank away from the malodorous man. Silurian could smell the putrid stench of sweat from where he sat.

The farmer glanced over his shoulder, surprised to see the large man where the girl had been. Raising his eyebrows at the large man, the farmer placed part of the girl's order on the table, gave the newcomer a slight nod, and turned back to assemble the rest of the order.

While the farmer worked away, Silurian watched the man sneak the girl's order into his pockets, and walk away.

Silurian gaped.

The farmer placed the remainder of the girl's order upon the table and frowned, wondering what had happened to the first part. He shot her an angry glare.

"Where'd ya put it?"

The girl's happy face transformed into panic. "But sir, I haven't stoled yer food. I don't know wer'd it git."

The farmer rounded the table so fast the girl fell to her bottom in her haste to escape his advance.

"Then why do ya run?"

Frightened, she covered her face with dirty hands and began to cry.

To Silurian's surprise, the big man reappeared out of the milling crowd and approached the table, a sadistic grin on his face. "There be a problem 'ere, good sir?"

The farmer placed his fists on his hips. "Aye, there be a problem." He pointed a sausage-sized finger at the weeping girl. "This lil bugger's gone and stole me wares from 'neath me nose."

"That so?" the large man said to the weeping girl. He shook his head. Placing a palm on his forehead, resting his elbow upon an upturned hand at his waist, he contemplated what to do. With an exasperated grunt, he slapped his thigh. "I don't know what I's ta do with this girl. I send her on a simple errand and she does this. This! Probably wanting ta keep a copper for herself, me thinks, eh?"

Silurian glanced at the table where the girl had placed her money. It was gone!

While the large man talked to the farmer, Silurian watched the weeping girl remove her hands from her stricken face and crab walk away from the two men, her eyes filled with terror. She would probably get a whipping, at the very least, for her transgression. Poor child.

"I tells ya what," the big man said. "How 'bout I look afta da bill?" He produced the very burlap money pouch the girl had placed upon the table earlier. "And I take her home an' teach her a lesson, eh? No harm done, eh? Whadya say?"

The farmer wasn't happy, but neither did he want trouble with the brute. Still, he had a business to run. "Thieves are to be losing a hand in these parts. I have a livin' to see to, ya know."

The large man held up his hands. "I hears ya. I hears ya. How's 'bout I throw in an extra copper fer yer troubles, eh? How's that soundin' t' ya?" He raised his eyebrows, giving the farmer a wink. "That way we all come away 'appy like."

"Well..." It was the farmer's turn to place a palm to his forehead. He sighed, "Okay. Just this once. Next time I give 'er over to the law."

The big man nodded with a grin and went to open the money pouch.

"Hey! Give that back! That's mine!"

Both men turned in time to see the girl running at them. She swiped at the purse, grasping only air as the big man lifted the pouch above his head. She jumped at the man's arm, but missed.

The man backhanded her across the face with his free hand, sending her sprawling to the dirt. Blood trickled from her nose.

The man began to count coppers into the farmer's upturned palm.

The girl sprang to her feet, and grabbed at the man's thick forearm. "You give it back!"

The brute grabbed her by the scruff of her tunic, pulling her backward. "I'll deal with ye soon 'nuff, lassie," he sniggered. "Now keep yer fool yip shut." He threw her so hard he nearly tore the shift from her body.

She landed in the path of a heavily laden wagon that had to swerve hard to miss her. The driver cussed her up one side and down the other for having the gall to be thrown in front of his cart. He could have broken a spoke turning so quick.

She sat up, buried her face in her hands, and cried, "...My money...Momma's gonna flay me...Dunno that man...My money..."

Silurian was heartsick. The poor girl. 'Momma's gonna flay her.' 'Doesn't know that man.' A creepy feeling tingled his skin. He recalled what those men wanted with Melody.

"What the...?" the big man exclaimed as Silurian snatched the pouch from his hand; the effort of doing so causing the money in the farmer's hand to fly into the air.

Before Silurian could take two steps, or even noticed the blade, he felt the cold steel thump flat against his spine. The impact threw him face first into the street, knocking the wind from his lungs. He lost his purchase on the little bag in the process, the money pouch jangling to a halt ahead of him, coming to rest in a mud puddle.

The little girl scrambled to her feet and pounced on the pouch, but before she could get up, a black leather boot stomped down hard. The large man bore his weight onto her delicate hand, threatening to break her little fingers.

She screamed in pain, wriggling and pulling to no avail. Getting to her knees, she bit the man's shin.

"Why you little—" the brute declared, raising his other foot to smash her insolent face.

"Hold!" a deep voice resonated behind the man, causing him to check his kick.

Many in the busy street had gathered around, enjoying the spectacle unfolding in the market. All eyes turned to the newcomer. Gasps escaped the lips of some, while others dropped to one knee, whispering, "The prince."

The large man's knuckles turned white, gripping his sword hard. His menacing glare displayed his hatred for the well-dressed young man striding confidently up to him. Flowing, golden locks denoted him as Prince Malcolm Svelte, heir to the Ivory Throne.

The large man spat on the ground. "Ye have no business here, Malcolm. Why don't ye go hunt some poor fox, or whatever other helpless creatures ye Spelts prey upon?"

The prince ignored the man's deliberate mispronunciation of his surname. He lifted his chin to indicate the girl on her knees. Tears smeared the filth coating her face. Her damaged fingers cradled the remnants of the muddy pouch. "As opposed to what? Surely you can best someone bigger than she."

Snickers rippled through the crowd.

The man cast an evil glance around him. The laughter stopped. He brought his glare to bear on the prince's deep blue eyes. "Ye should hold yer tongue in these parts, I'd say. Ye are nae welcome amongst us lower class tripe, I'm thinking. If ye're not careful, ye might find it is ye who is bested."

Gasps rippled amongst the crowd.

Malcolm took a deliberate breath. He turned his attention to the farmer who watched on with indifference, large forearms folded across his chest.

"Hail to you, good merchant. Tell me what event has brought the fine people of Cliff Face to a standstill?" Malcolm spread his arms, turning first one way, and then the other, to include the rapidly growing crowd.

The farmer gave the large man a sidelong glance before responding, "Well, me liege…" He gave an account of the events as he saw them, including the girl's apparent theft.

The large man rocked on his heels as the farmer related the story. A smug look crossed his face at the mention of the theft and the unsolicited intervention of the stupid whelp sitting in the street trying to catch his breath.

Prince Malcolm gave Silurian a fleeting glance.

"There ye go, Mister Zephyr." The large man spat on the ground. "Now why don' ye leave us common folk alone an' go raze a country or something."

Titters filtered throughout the mob.

Prince Malcolm stroked his blonde mustache. He stepped to the girl's side. Kneeling before her, he inspected her battered hand. "Is that how it happened, little miss?"

The girl, overwhelmed by the whole incident, pulled her hand away, shaking her head.

Prince Malcolm stood up to face the farmer. "The girl denies your story."

The farmer unfolded his arms, spreading them wide. "Me liege, all I know is what happened. I placed her order on the table, turned me back, and it be gone."

The prince looked from the farmer to the girl dressed in rags, barely hiding her bony frame. "And she's hiding these vegetables, where?"

The farmer became flustered. "I don't exactly know, me Lord. All I knows is what happened."

"Perhaps I can help, sire." Silurian stood up, dusting off his clothes.

The large man growled, baring his teeth, "Off with you whelp, afore I whack you with the edge of me sword."

Wary, Silurian walked up to the prince and took a knee. Staring at the ground, he declared, "I saw everything, my Lord."

The large man kicked Silurian in the ribs, knocking him to the ground, gasping for breath.

Before Silurian hit the street, Prince Malcolm's sword was beneath the brute's chin, a metallic ring slowly dissipating into the air.

The crowd held its breath.

"If you strike another one of my subjects without my consent you'll wish you were the fox," Malcolm snarled, his face inches from the big man's. "Understand? Tripe?"

The man glared death at the young prince.

After a few tense moments, the prince lowered his sword. With an eye on the man, he bent at the knees to offer Silurian a hand. "Are you alright?"

Silurian attempted a brave smile. Swallowing his discomfort at speaking to a real, live member of the House of Svelte, he said, "Aye, my liege. I'll live, I reckon." He gripped the prince's hand and gained his feet, hugging his bruised ribs.

The large man grunted his displeasure and spat, barely missing Silurian's shabby boots.

The prince gave the brute a disgusted look, and addressed Silurian, "What is your name?"

"Silurian, my lord. Silurian Mintaka, son of Zorn."

Zorn? Zorn Mintaka? He had heard that name before. Recently, in fact, but for the life of him he couldn't place it. "It's alright, son of Zorn. Speak your piece. You needn't fear this man."

Silurian's eyes darted between the prince's blue eyes and the ruffian's veined glare. "I, well, I mean her," he struggled, intimidated by the brute.

The large man growled, the left side of his mouth baring chipped, yellow teeth.

Silurian gulped. "The little girl there," he pointed, "well, she ordered vegetables from the farmer. All of a sudden, this man comes along," he couldn't bring himself to point, "and talks with the farmer. When the farmer turned away, he stole the vegetables." He winced, expecting to be hit again.

The prince considered the fidgeting man in question. "What of it, man? Does the boy have the truth of the matter?"

The man spat again, discomfort twisting his expression. "I imagine ye have already decided that of yer own accord. The real truth of the matter will be put to the sword, I do nae doubt. I was guilty in yer eyes afore ya ever tried me. What good is me word to one as righteous as ye?"

The prince shook his head. "No. I cannot convict you on the sole testimony of a young boy."

The large man grinned.

The prince stroked the corners of his mouth. There was no possible way the girl could be hiding anything in her threadbare attire.

"Empty your pockets," Malcolm said calmly.

The large man gaped. "What?"

"You heard me. Empty your pockets."

The man shook his head, outraged. Eyeing the prince's sword, he turned the pockets in his breeches inside out. Dirt and lint fell to the street.

The prince smiled. "And the pockets lining your tunic."

The man shook his head in disgust. Again, he turned out empty pockets.

The prince rubbed his lower lip with a loose fist, at a loss on to how to proceed. Malcolm had little doubt the man lied, but without evidence, he had no authority to condemn him.

The brute sheathed his sword. "Now, if ye don't suspect me of witchcraft, I shall be on me way." He shouldered past Malcolm, showing no regard for the money left on the table. He stole a quick glance at Silurian, a look that promised the boy he would rue this day.

The prince pursed his lips in thought. Why would the man walk away and leave his money on the table? He considered the girl. She couldn't have hidden the vegetables, but he knew the farmer would demand retribution. It was plain she could ill afford to pay for something she hadn't received.

"Say, good farmer, how much—"

"Sire!" Silurian pointed to a gap in the crowd.

Malcolm turned in time to see the large man grab a bulging sack from a tall, skinny man leaning against a dun coloured building across the street.

Malcolm scowled, setting off with large strides. "Hey! You two! Stop!"

The large man offered the prince a cavalier smile and bolted away.

Elusive

Silurian snapped out of his reverie. He could still feel the bruises the brute had inflicted on his ribs and the small of his back.

Standing upon the edge of a small bluff, Melody and Silurian peered through the deluge at the sprawling buildings of Cliff Face below. The storm had beaten them to the derelict city.

The northernmost outpost in Zephyr lay nestled behind the confines of a wooden battlement. The only breach in the fortification, a solitary gate. Two stone towers flanked an iron portcullis, guarding the main road's approach.

Lightning lashed the sky over the city. The ensuing thunder reverberated throughout the valley basin between Mount Cinder and Mount Gloom, both peaks lost in the roiling clouds.

"How's your shoulder?" Melody asked, her heart racing in response to the storm's fury, her anxiety rising with their proximity to the city.

Lightning flashed.

Silurian waited for the long rumble of thunder to pass. "It's sore. Here, let me tuck your hair in."

She gathered her hair together, grimacing as he stuffed the long strands inside her tunic. Cold water streamed down her back, reaching her nether regions.

Silurian considered his sister's bulging hair with a resigned sigh. "Let's go. Stay close, and whatever you do, don't talk to anybody. Understand?"

She followed her brother's receding backside, muttering more to herself, "Ya, ya, ya. You said that a hundred times already. I'm not stupid."

"Ya, well just don't forget," he said without looking back.

Approaching the gate, they were relieved to find the guards absent; likely huddled over a tankard of mead, out of the rain. A small wagon train, urged on by sodden, grim-faced merchants, provided them cover. They walked up to the rearmost wagon, kept pace with it until well past the gatehouse, and slipped away unseen into a dark alleyway.

Lightning lit up the sky.

"Now what?" Melody asked, glancing around, trying to discern the alley's far end through the downpour.

"Keep your voice down," Silurian whispered. "We have to find somebody who needs help."

He peeked out of the alley, scanning the muddy street.

Melody put her mouth close to Silurian's ear. "There aren't many people out. What if we can't find anyone to help? What then?" Her voice cracked with fright. "Oh, Sil. I'm so hungry. And cold."

"Ya. Me too. Don't worry. I've done this for months. We haven't starved yet, have we?"

"No." Shivers wracked her frail body, causing her voice to tremble. She added, more testily than she meant to, "But we have gone to bed hungry more nights than I care to remember."

As soon as the words left her lips, she regretted them. Her brother worked tirelessly to provide for them. Scrounging, begging, and helping people from all walks of life. Many times, all he received for his effort was a black eye or a fat lip as payment for some backbreaking service he'd performed the entire day. He never once complained.

She expected to see an expression of hurt on his face, but her words hadn't fazed him at all. He just smiled and patted her nearest forearm to comfort her.

The wind diminished within the walled city. Lightning etched jagged paths across the churning clouds, heralding ground-shaking thunderclaps that reverberated into the distance.

With the advent of the storm, Silurian knew the pickings would be slim in this area of town. The more affluent citizens of Cliff Face would not be caught wandering about in the muck. If they wanted to find work, they needed to travel to the seedier district. There, the rain would simply provide the peddlers with a much-needed bath. They were more likely to be taken advantage of in the lower end of town, but given the weather, what choice did they have?

"At the far end of this alley is a street that leads to the market. Stay behind me." Silurian scanned the road they had come in on once more before hastening down the alleyway in the opposite direction, the noise of their splashing footsteps lost in the din of pelting rain.

From the shelter of a darkened doorway, a bearded visage watched two rain-soaked figures dart into an alleyway. The taller of the two peered out a few times before scampering out of sight. There was something familiar about that one.

He stepped out from the shadows, surveyed the deserted street, and eased his huge frame into the alley.

Lightning illuminated the rain drenched, wooden buildings on either side as they approached the alley's far end.

"Geez, Mel," Silurian breathed. "You almost knocked me into the street."

"Well sor—ry! I didn't realize you were going to suddenly grow roots." Her words lost in the ensuing thunderclap.

Silurian braced himself against the corner of a rundown tenement on the alley's left side. He watched a ramshackle wagon with odd-sized, wobbly wheels slogging its way through the muck. The irate driver cursed his underfed mule—the beast's back curving bowl-like from protruding shoulder blades to bony hips.

Peering up the street to his left, Silurian noted many rundown businesses. Signs in various states of disrepair creaked above doorways to taverns and cobbler shops, smithies and houses of not so respectable repute. During nicer days, the street would be lined with sagging tables laden with goods. Today, even in this area of Cliff Face, the street entertained only the splattering rain as it created thousands of pockmarks in the muck.

His attention fell on the wagon. Stopped in the middle of the street, the mule refused to take another step in the deep mud.

The driver jumped from his seat, issuing a barrage of colourful language. He promptly lost his footing and fell onto his rump with a noisy slap.

Silurian bit his tongue. Melody's fingers dug into his sides, a muffled guffaw forcing its way through her clenched teeth. Silurian elbowed her in the ribs.

Cursing louder, the rider got to his feet, wiped at the muck caked to his posterior, and kicked the mule hard in the stomach. The poor animal lurched forward, braying at the sky. The wagon's front corner caught the rider square in the back, knocking him face first into a puddle. The mule continued trudging down the street.

An audible chortle escaped the siblings' lips. Horrified, they covered their mouths.

The man whipped his head in their direction and rose unsteadily to his feet. Squinting, he watched them withdraw deeper into the alley.

"Come on outta there! I sees ya spying on me!" Lightning flashed, illuminating them as plain as day.

The fear in his sister's eyes matched Silurian's own. He grabbed her by the forearm, about to drag her down the alley, when he spotted the furtive movement of something large approaching from the opposite end.

He considered fleeing up the alley anyway, but when the cloaked figure backed into the shadows, he changed his mind. Swallowing the lump in his throat, he pulled his sister into the street toward the irate wagon rider. Fumbling inside his tunic, he grasped the handle of his crude hunting knife.

The rider stormed over to them, slipping twice, before his foul-smelling form bumped into Silurian's chest, knocking him backward into Melody.

"What's da big idear a-spying on a poor ol', honest merchant, trying to get his ornery animal an' truck outta da rain?"

Silurian gaped at the mention of the man's ornery animal, and found himself staring into the man's wrinkled visage, noting the wretch's crooked, yellow tooth.

"Sorry, sir. We were in the alley and saw you tending your wagon. We meant you no harm."

The merchant snorted, spraying him with spittle. He jabbed Silurian in the chest with a bony finger. "Ain't your parents a-teaching you manners, boy? Ain't they a-telling you it's rude to spy on people? Especially *honest* people like meself."

"We're sorry sir. We didn't mean to spy on you."

"Then why do you lurk in that there hidey-hole, huh?" The merchant drove his finger into Silurian's chest so hard he knocked him back a step.

Silurian stepped on his sister's foot, causing her to cry out in pain.

The merchant's attention went to her. He squinted, studying her face, paying particular attention to the hair bulging around her collar.

Silurian peered around him. "Your wagon! It's getting away!"

"What?" The merchant turned in time to see the wagon disappear around the corner of the next intersection, half a block away. "Why that dirty little…"

The man's words were lost to them as Silurian grabbed his sister's arm and pulled her away. "Come on."

Together they scampered after the wagon, Melody struggling to keep up in the sloppy conditions.

Silurian waited for her at the intersection. "Let's catch his mule."

Melody looked at him like his hair was on fire. "Have you gone mad?"

The merchant's colourful language followed them down the street as he slipped and stumbled in their wake.

From the cover of the alleyway, the cloaked figure watched the confrontation between the scrawny man and his hapless quarry. The rain had lessened, and during a lightning flash, he also took note of the smaller one's bulging hair. A smile crossed his thin lips.

Silurian and Melody caught sight of the rogue wagon through the lessening rainfall, and started after it. Melody fell behind again, but was in no danger of being caught by the merchant.

It wasn't long before Silurian passed the wagon and grabbed the mule's dangling rein. Pulling hard, he managed to stop it. Coming around the corner behind them, the merchant cussed incomprehensibly.

Melody caught up, gasping for breath, her muddied right-side evidence of a fall. Wiping at the straggling hair clinging to her face, she said, "Come on. We stopped the wagon, let's run."

"Here. Let me tuck your hair in."

She gathered her hair. Taking it from her, he jammed the unruly tresses into her tunic, keeping an eye on the merchant as the disgruntled man plodded uncertainly toward them, scowling.

Silurian gave her hair a final tuck. "Here he comes," he whispered. "Remember, not a word."

If they thought the merchant had exhausted his repertoire of obscenities, they were mistaken. "What's the meaning of running off 'n me? I oughta tan your britches." He made a move toward them, his right hand raised.

"But, sir," Silurian implored. "We caught your mule."

"Humph," the rider snorted, spitting, barely missing the boy's shabby footwear. "Wouldna gitten far in this storm." He wrenched the reins from Silurian's grasp and proceeded to kick the mule in the ribs. The animal brayed at the sky, attempting to move again, but the man viciously pulled on the reins, causing the metal bit to rattle on its teeth.

"And just why are two young…" He cast an inquisitive gaze at Melody, recalling what he suspected earlier. His eyes narrowed, "…two young kids out here in the storm? No decent folk'd allow their younguns out on a day like this."

"Uh," Silurian said, thinking fast, "we were running an errand on the far side of town when the storm caught us. We were on our way home when we came upon you, and—"

"Humph." The rider hacked and spat. "I don't reckon I believes ya. But ain't no matter." He squinted his eyes, enthralled with Melody's hair. "I think there's more to yous two than meets the eye, hmm?"

He took a step toward Melody, reaching out to grab her shoulders.

Silurian pointed. "Your wagon's on fire!"

"What the...?"

Silurian grabbed Melody's arm and dragged her after him. "We're outta here."

She didn't need to be told twice. It was all he could do to keep up with her.

The merchant cussed them with a raised fist, but didn't follow.

From his vantage point at the intersection, partially hidden behind a tavern's porch sign, the grizzled man watched the antics in the street. His weathered mien was marred by a scar running up his right cheek that began below his lip and extended clear through the centre of his right eye—the ruined eye hidden behind a black leather patch. His prey fled from the sad sack wagon owner hopelessly embedded in the quagmire of a street.

He eyed the smaller one's neck, no longer suspicious of her gender.

He squinted to keep the slowing rain from his good eye. His quarry disappeared down another alley, but no matter. His knowledge of the recesses and secret byways of Cliff Face allowed him to smile. Without a care in the world he slid off the porch and around the intersection the way he had come.

He couldn't believe his good fortune. He knew that boy, and the boy owed him. A lot.

It promised to be a good night.

The Fatal Damsel

"It's okay," Silurian panted. "He didn't follow us."

He peeked around the corner of the noisy building they hid behind. Muffled music and raucous laughter sounded from within. Satisfied they were safe, he pulled back into the alley, smiling at his forlorn sister.

Misreading his thoughts, she moaned, "Yay, we outran an out of shape, crotchety, old man. Wow. That doesn't change the fact that we are cold. Or hungry."

Silurian reached into his pockets, withdrawing a shiny red apple in each hand. "Ta da."

"Where did you get those?"

Tossing one to her, he winked and took a bite out of his, mischief written all over his face.

Her mouth dropped open. She glanced past him to the street beyond, expecting to see the farmer. "You stole them. How could you?"

Silurian tried to smile through a mouthful of apple. He mumbled, "Relax. I took them from the wagon." He swallowed and winked. "Payment for catching it."

She mulled over his explanation until her hunger got the better of her. She broke the skin with her teeth and ravenously devoured the apple's meat. While she ate, the rain abated further. Shivering uncontrollably, her sodden clothing clinging to her slight body, she stuffed the apple core into her pocket. Their next meal might be a long time coming.

Silurian stashed his core as well and looked to the sky. The rain had stopped. Perhaps their fortunes were turning. With any luck, in a couple of hours, the merchants would start selling their wares in the marketplace and be in need of their services.

The noise from the tavern rose in conjunction with the rapidly disappearing clouds. Silurian read the weathered sign hanging above the saloon doors: *The Fatal Damsel*. It wouldn't be long before the revelry inside spilled out into the street. He didn't want Mel anywhere nearby when that happened.

They slipped into the street, quickly putting distance between themselves and the tavern.

Sliding unseen into the far end of the alley, the scar-faced man nodded, pleased with himself. His knowledge of the city had not let him down. At the alley's far end he spotted his quarry huddled within the shadows. His lopsided harelip curled up in delight. He could almost taste the sweetness of his thoughts.

A sudden shout from the street behind him distracted him for only a moment, but by the time he looked back, they were gone. He ran up the alley as fast as his huge frame would carry him.

Boisterous laughter greeted him at the far end. His blood pressure soared. Four men stood upon the dilapidated porch fronting *The Fatal Damsel.* Were they laughing at him? Nobody laughed at him. Not if they wished to walk again. He was about to break some heads when the men, oblivious of his presence, laughed at something the shortest man said.

Taking a few deep breaths to calm himself, he snorted his derision and scanned the street. His prize was nowhere to be seen. The scarred corner of his lip lifted in an angered sneer, his gaze darting everywhere at once. Unsure of which way he should go in search of his prey, it dawned on him the four men had suddenly become quiet.

He whipped his head in their direction, smelling a strong odour of liquor. His good eye squinted. The four men were staring at him like he was some kind of freak. Oh, he was used to it. Especially now, with his beautiful complexion ruined by that awful scar.

He leered at them. "An' jus' what ye be looking at?"

The biggest man elbowed the companion next to him, aping the grizzled man, "An' jus' what ye be looking at?"

His companions roared.

Encouraged, the speaker placed a hand over one eye. "Why, by the looks of ye, I dare say, not much."

The speaker let forth a belly laugh. Looking to his friends for support, he was surprised at the stricken expressions upon their faces. They weren't laughing. They were stepping backward, away from the man.

The speaker whirled about. He, too, lost his grin.

"Whew. That was close," Silurian said tending his sister's loose strands. They had taken refuge around the next intersection.

Standing on a wooden porch, fronting a rundown livery, Melody and Silurian debated their next move. The squeal of rusty hinges diverted Silurian's attention back the way they had come.

The front doors of *The Fatal Damsel* banged open, and the quelled din they heard earlier spilled into the street. Four men stumbled through the swinging doors and staggered to a stop at the entrance to the alley, where another person skulked about in the shadows. Someone large.

Without another thought, Silurian pulled Melody from the porch.

They made their way up a muddy side street, taking advantage of odd stretches of unstable sidewalk when they could, the wooden slats broken or missing more often than not. At the next intersection, they stopped on a short span of mud-splattered boards.

Not happy with her hair, he turned Melody by the shoulders and gathered her loose strands, stuffing them into her collar. The image of the man in the alley, though it had been nothing but a silhouette, unsettled him. There was something familiar about their stalker. Something more than just his earlier sighting of him.

Melody's voice interrupted his thoughts. Shaking his head to rid himself of the uneasy feeling, he said, "Huh?"

Pulling free of his attending hands, she faced him. "I said, deaf-o, what do we do now?"

"I—uh, I'm not sure." He struggled to push the images from his mind. "I guess we can walk around Cliff Face for a while. Perhaps help out in the nicer marketplace if the sun dries up the muck."

She agreed they needed to escape the rougher part of town. She had almost screamed at the last intersection when she saw the four men stagger out of *The Fatal Damsel*. Even now she breathed heavier than normal.

Although this particular street wasn't exactly in the seedier part of Cliff Face, it served as a buffer between the regular marketplace and the city's shantytown. The eastern half of Cliff Face housed the baron and his household army, as well as those of more affluent persuasion.

They would stand out amongst the upper-class citizens in all their finery and smelling of washed, perfumed bodies. The prospect of being hired along the eastern thoroughfares wouldn't be as good, considering their clothing. They would more than likely be shunned as beggars, but at least it would be safer.

Silurian wasn't happy with his sister's hair. He fussed with the strands that had come loose. Giving her a once over, he sighed in resignation, "Alright, you ready?"

Ensuring the way was clear, he set off along the sloppy road to their right. "This way."

As Melody kept pace behind him, she thought he muttered, "I think."

Royal Encounter

By the time the sun vanquished the storm over the eastern mountain peak of Mount Gloom, it had already begun its descent into the western sky. Soon Cliff Face would fall under Mount Cinder's shadow.

A gentle breeze chilled the siblings as they meandered along a grassy thoroughfare, their clothes still damp from the morning rain. A vine-covered, stone wall loomed in the distance, encompassing the baron's homestead. The residence proper rested high upon a hill, commanding a view of the entire city.

Alone with their thoughts, they dreamed of another life. A fantasy life.

Melody smiled. In her mind, she frolicked along the baron's shaded paths. Her parents sat upon a bench, holding hands—

"Hey," a fully armoured knight, astride a great warhorse, called out. He approached them from behind so fast neither teenager had noticed him. "Make way."

The rider kicked out with his steel-plated boot, shoving Silurian into Melody, causing them to stumble over themselves.

Silurian fell to the ground, but he was able to support Melody long enough for her to regain her balance. He was about to protest, but the rider's surcoat and the matching one draped over his mount, made him bite his tongue. The rider's colours, and indeed those of the pennant fluttering from the standard he bore, signified the king's house: a golden eagle, wings poised for landing, clenching a sword within hooked talons, all upon a vermillion background.

From beneath his raised faceplate, the black bearded knight reined in his horse and snarled, "On your knees, vermin. Can't you see you are in the presence of Prince Malcolm, heir to the Ivory Throne?" The man's free hand swept behind him, indicating the small entourage of riders following. All the riders in the parade still wore their conical helms, except two.

Silurian looked quickly at the two bareheaded men, his mind racing with what his father had told him about the royal house of Zephyr. The pennant bearer's actions bespoke of a cruel overlord, but his father had always spoken highly of the Svelte family. Prince Malcolm's actions in the marketplace a month ago had certainly supported that view.

Silurian grabbed Melody's wrist, pulling her to her knees. She cast him a dirty look, only to see his head bowed in respect. She stole a quick glance at the passing knights who were reining in their mounts, and did likewise.

Silence gripped the street. The only sounds were those of songbirds roosting in the trees, and snorting horses with jingling tack, and the occasional clop of shod hooves as a restless steed adjusted its stance. Citizens walking along the street stopped what they were doing and took a knee.

The prince motioned the onlookers to their feet and on their way. With heads bowed, they complied.

In unison, Melody and Silurian stole a peek and were immediately abashed to find themselves gazing into the prince's warm, blue eyes.

Towering above them, mounted on a magnificent white stallion, the prince smiled; his mustachioed face surrounded by wavy locks of blonde hair cascading about his burnished, golden breastplate. They gasped and lowered their gaze to the ground.

The prince laughed, "Arise, young ones."

Rising timidly to their feet, they kept their gaze locked upon an imaginary spot on the ground. Silurian had met the prince already, but this encounter felt a lot more formal than it had in the marketplace.

Again, the prince laughed, this time joined by his men. All but the pennant bearer.

"It's okay. You may look upon me." He waited patiently as the two eyed each other.

Hoping they wouldn't be mistreated again, they gazed into the prince's eyes, finding nothing but warmth and compassion.

The prince sensed the younger child's fear of him. With a grim smile, he said, "I apologize for the actions of my knight." He held a cupped hand conspiratorially over his mouth, and winked, "I shall deal with him later."

Melody and Silurian offered him a faint smile.

Prince Malcolm considered the wet, grimy, forlorn teenagers quaking before him. Likely from the shantytown on the far side of Cliff Face, living in squalor. Perhaps their father had been killed serving the baron in the king's name? Whatever their story, his heart went out to them.

His own father, the king, had tried to instill in him the fact that kings must steel themselves to the knowledge that many of their subjects were destined to live in poverty. An heir to the throne had to accept the fact they could not change the world. No matter how hard they tried to change the system, people would always find a way to live in squalor. His father drove home these lessons repeatedly. If Malcolm wished to ascend the Ivory Throne, he needed to grow a thicker hide.

Prince Malcolm recalled these lessons as he pondered the blatant destitution before him, but he couldn't help his feelings if their apparent lot in life broke his heart. Surely, as prince, he must be able to do something. Besides, the king wasn't here. It would be years before he needed to worry himself over ascending the Ivory Throne.

"Do you live around here?"

Neither child spoke. They lowered their heads, ashamed.

The pennant bearer cleared his throat, about to say something harsh, but Prince Malcolm silenced him with a raised hand.

Observing the teenagers bowed heads, Malcolm noticed the smaller one's hair disappearing into the back of her tunic.

"It's okay, you may speak. Do you, or your sister," at the mention of 'sister', Silurian's head whipped around to her, and then up at the smiling prince, "want something to eat?"

Silurian stared at the prince in disbelief. He started to sputter something incomprehensible, but was cut short by his sister's squeak.

"Oh, yes sir. I-I mean, my Lord Prince." Embarrassed, Melody put a hand to her mouth, surprised she had spoken at all.

Smiling at her response, Malcolm studied the boy. He was doubtless charged with the girl's safety. He sensed by the boy's demeanour that he took this responsibility seriously. Malcolm admired that.

The prince motioned to the other young man whose helm rested upon his saddle's pommel. "Good squire, Jarr-nash. Gather up a satchel of whatever food we have left."

Malcolm's squire rolled his eyes, mocking his liege's good heartedness, "Aye, sir young and noble prince. 'Tis a good thing for you that your father isn't here."

The prince returned Jarr-nash's smile, muttering under his breath, "Tis a good thing he won't be hearing about this either, isn't it?"

Jarr-nash laughed and went about the business of collecting their remaining stores. Most riders obliged at once without comment, but a couple of the older, gruffer knights, the pennant bearer included, begrudgingly obeyed their lord's request.

While the collection took place, Prince Malcolm returned his attention to Melody and Silurian. There was something familiar about them. The boy, for sure.

"Whereabouts do you two call home?"

Silurian avoided eye contact. "We live over there, sir. I mean, my Lord Prince." He pointed west.

"Prince will do," Malcolm smiled. "What brings you two so far from home?"

Thinking quickly, Silurian partially told the truth, ashamed of purposely misleading a prince. "We went for a walk, my prince. After such a long storm, we wanted to get outside, so we decided to see this part of Cliff Face. I know," he lowered his head, "we shouldn't be in this part of town."

Malcolm didn't know how to respond to that. He watched the progress of his squire as the grumpy pennant bearer reluctantly handed over his scant food supplies. He needed to have a serious talk with that one.

Searching for something to say, he asked, "What are your names?"

Silurian scuffed his right foot in the dirt, wondering how to respond. Not wanting to rouse the prince's suspicions, he forced himself to smile. "I-I am Silurian Mintaka, son of Zorn Mintaka of Cliff Face." He raised his head, proclaiming his father's name with pride. "And this is Mel…" he paused, but remembered the prince had already guessed, "…ody, daughter of Mase Storms End. Niece of Lord Therin of Storms End."

Recognition lit upon the prince's face. "I knew it. You are the boy from the marketplace. The one who stood up to save a little girl from a horrible fate."

"Yes sir, that was me."

Malcolm stared long and hard at Melody, chin in hand. "Surely this can't be her?"

"No, my prince. Melody wasn't with me."

"I didn't think so. Melody here is much too pretty to be the same girl."

Silurian smiled. He was but a lowly peasant, and yet, the prince had remembered him.

"Well, in any case, I ask you to accept a gift from the royal house of Zephyr as an apology for the treatment you received by the foot of one of my men."

The prince's squire finished gathering two satchels of food and walked over to stand patiently beside his liege, listening to Malcolm address the youngsters.

Melody and Silurian looked on incredulously, unable to speak. Together they stared up at the angelic figure before them.

Jarr-nash leaned forward to whisper clumsily behind a hand burdened by one of the satchels, "What about the sacks, sire?"

"What of them?" The prince frowned. "Surely they cannot carry their truck without satchels."

"As you wish, my lord," Jarr-nash responded, handing a leather bag to each child.

When Jarr-nash had remounted, Malcolm donned his plated, chain-link greaves as the grateful siblings struggled to hold onto their loads. "Tell your parents they eat courtesy of house Svelte tonight."

Giving them a wink, he spurred away. As an afterthought, he said over his shoulder, "By the way, I caught the brute responsible for the trouble in the market that day. I dare say he won't be causing trouble around here anytime soon."

Quarry Lost

A mischievous grin split the man's grizzled face. He had been right to backtrack to the main street exiting the city. He knew most people in the lower section of town, and he couldn't recall ever seeing his quarry there before. With the inhabitants of Cliff Face out in full force he had given up hope of finding them again, but at last his patience was rewarded. Coming straight down the street, headed for the city gates, were the two people he sought. The smaller one hiding her femininity.

He slunk into the shadows of a recessed doorway. He estimated the boy to be around fifteen or sixteen, the girl a year or two younger. They each clung tightly to a leather sack as they made their way into the crowd milling about the gatehouse. They were likely heading home with the provisions their parents had requested; the children of farmers, who, upon seeing the morning was going to be a washout, had sent them into town instead of helping out on the farm. Oh well. They wouldn't be going home today. Or any other day, for that matter. He would dispatch the boy without much difficulty, something he should have done a few weeks earlier before that whoreson prince had shown his ugly face.

And the girl. Oh, the girl. She would compensate quite nicely for the grievous harm he had received as a result of the prince's so-called justice. He would take her to his secluded cabin on Mount Gloom. He could see it all now. He almost drooled.

Squinting to better see his quarry in the shadowy street, he realized that if he didn't start after them soon, he might lose them again. They were already funneling through the open gatehouse, disappearing amongst the throng beyond.

He wiped the perspiration from his brow. The air was stale, close and humid, compounded by the congestion of so many people in the street. Shouldering his way past the dumb people lollygagging before the barbican, he stepped onto the dirt road.

His chest constricted. Where were they?

He forced himself to breathe. They would be outside the gates.

Curses followed his progress to the gatehouse. He greeted the malcontents by tossing them out of his way.

"Hey, mister," a burly farmer fumed as the grizzled man knocked his wife to the ground. "Ye'll answer for—" The farmer grabbed the scarred man's left forearm just in time to meet a bone-crushing fist. Blood spurted beneath the farmer's hands as he cupped his broken nose, sitting stunned upon the street.

The crowd in the immediate area parted for the big man after witnessing the brutal demonstration. No one wished anything to do with him.

The grizzled man held his tender knuckles as he bullied his way through the gatehouse proper. Outside the city gates he stopped and stared. People walked around him grumbling that he hadn't the decency to at least step to the side, but he didn't care. His treasure was gone. Vanished. How could that be?

He ran along the path for several minutes, inspecting anyone vaguely resembling his prey. He received many strange stares and offhanded remarks about his behaviour. He was oblivious to them all. When one of the braver men approached him, he threw the man aside like an absent thought.

The crowded path narrowed. He stopped, scanning the valley floor. They were gone.

Dropping to his knees, his strange behaviour caused passersby to give him a wide berth. Unconcerned with the spectacle he was creating, he pounded the ground with clenched fists. Raising his arms over his head he stared skyward, emitting a yell of such frustration it surely would have triggered an avalanche had the season been right.

The maniacal roar echoed amongst the surrounding peaks, before dissipating into the distance.

Silurian pulled the bunched-up poultice from beneath his tunic and threw it under the pine tree they sat beside, its usefulness long since expired.

Melody pulled open his tunic's neck, frowning at the festering claw marks—typical of troll inflicted wounds.

Shrugging her off, he rose to his feet and started up the trail along Mount Cinder's shoulder.

A mournful wail reached their ears, reverberating along the heights, giving them goosebumps.

Melody flinched at the dreadful keening, searching all about, expecting some beast to come crashing through the undergrowth.

Shaking off the feeling, she freed her hair from its itchy confinement. It had irritated her terribly during the day. Even now, vestiges of moisture still clung to her scalp as a result of the morning's storm. She ran her fingers through the infinite tangles. "Ah. Free again."

Silurian stopped to wait, offering her a brief smile. "Come on. We better make tracks if we want to find shelter before dark."

Melody withdrew her fingers from her hair, stretching her arms in a long yawn. Speaking, her words sounded long and hollow, "Why can't we just stay under this pine? I'm so tired I don't think my feet will walk any more. Even if I ask them politely."

Silurian grunted, "I don't know about you, but I'd rather not become some creature's midnight snack."

She let her arms drop to her side, defeated. "Surely the night animals won't dare come this close to Cliff Face. If they do, we can run to the gates. Ask for help." She stared at the ground, trying her best to look pitiful.

"Use your head. Why do you think they lower the gate at night? To keep the people in? To break the wind?" He gestured at Mount Cinder rising into the blackening sky behind them. "This whole mountainside will soon be crawling with creatures we don't want to meet. Trolls will be the least of our worries."

His gaze wandered to the dizzying heights of Mount Gloom across the valley. "I don't even want to know what lurks up there."

Melody stomped the ground in frustration. "Why can't we stay in Cliff Face then?" Tears left tracks on her dirty face.

"Seriously? We've been over this again, and again, and again. You know you're not safe on the streets at night. Even if we found a hidey-hole, there's no guarantee we wouldn't be sharing it. If we know where the hidey-hole is, you can be sure others do too."

He picked up his sack, but put it back down again to embrace her. She was hurting. Scared. He knew she felt lonely and abandoned by the world. She probably felt pity for herself—at the way life had betrayed her, robbing her of her possessions, her lifestyle, her home. Her parents. He knew her lust for life kept sinking lower with each passing day. He knew it well. Life had dealt him the same hand.

She clung to him and wept. The tighter he held her the more she cried. She cried harder than she usually did each night before falling asleep. Their window of daylight was quickly fading, but he knew she needed to cleanse herself before they could carry on.

At sixteen, he was developing muscles he didn't know he had. Fate and circumstance were conspiring to have him mature quicker than most boys his age. Physically and mentally. He knew when to stand and fight and when to bow to the pressures placed upon him. His sister wasn't there yet. He had to be careful not to lose her. He was prepared to stand there all night if need be.

When her sobs eased to a whimper, she withdrew from his embrace. Wiping her cheeks and runny nose on a frayed cuff, she smeared the day's grime into ghastly swatches. Inhaling deeply to compose herself, she tried to sound brave, "How do I look?"

Silurian chuckled, "Awful."

As soon as the words left his mouth he wished them back.

Her hopeful face fell. She was on the verge of crying again.

Great, he thought. "I'm just funnin' ya. You're as pretty as an apple blossom."

"Really?"

"Really. Now get your bag and have a chat with those stubborn feet of yours. If we don't get back soon, Hairy's going to get worried."

Melody spit out a laugh. Only Silurian could cheer her up when she felt this low. She sniffled loudly, hefted her bag over her shoulder, and followed her brother up the barely distinguishable path leading to Mount Cinder's higher regions.

While they walked they kept their own council. At one point, Silurian found a short length of branch to use for a torch. He withdrew a length of oil-soaked cloth from a pouch he kept on his belt and wrapped it around one end of the stick.

Twilight suffused the mountainside with spooky shadows. The higher they climbed, the fewer trees they encountered. The day's rain induced a sweet smell from the scrubby groundcover. The surly sea below was lost in the gathering dusk to their right; the rising moon's reflection, far off on the horizon, the only indication of the water's existence. Everywhere else, the heights rose in stark relief against a darkening sky.

Silurian kept a careful watch. A sense of foreboding pricked the back of his consciousness. Night creatures undoubtedly tracked their progress, licking their lips.

Melody trudged along quietly, a few paces behind. Several times he slowed his pace, allowing her to catch up, only to have her fall behind again. Realizing she never actually fell too far behind, he kept walking, eating the food from his sack as he went.

Melody's voice caused him to stumble, so intent was he watching the terrain for phantom creatures.

"I can't walk anymore."

Silurian stopped.

She caught up to him and carelessly dropped her sack. Sitting heavily upon the ground, she stared at the grass between her feet. "My blisters are killing me. My legs are dead. Can't we just sit awhile?"

Silurian looked out over the void where the sea should have been, clenching his fists. He wanted to shout at her. With a measure of restraint evident in his voice, he said, “We’re almost at the first cave. We won’t be safe until we reach it.”

When she didn’t respond, he tucked the unlit torch under his armpit and picked up her sack. He offered her his other hand. “Come on. I’m hurting too. It’s not much farther.”

Melody stood without a word, letting her brother carry her sack. Together they climbed the rock-strewn trail toward the first cave Silurian had found for them over a month ago. The first cave they had encountered Hairy in.

When Melody recognized the boulder hiding the cave’s entrance, she stopped. “Wait.”

“What now?”

“This is where Hairy almost caught us.”

Silurian was thinking the same thing. He needed to be brave for her sake. “He has almost caught us in every cave. If we’re lucky, he’s still waiting for us in the other one.” *I hope.* “That cave is leagues from here.” As an afterthought, he added, “Trolls are pretty stupid.”

Melody wasn’t convinced.

It dawned on her how dark it had become. A distant howl grabbed her attention. Taking Silurian’s shirt by the shoulder, she dragged him toward the boulder. “Come on. Don’t just stand there, let’s go.”

Luckily the shoulder she grabbed wasn’t the injured one, but the sudden tightness of the garment still caused him pain. Not wanting to break his sister’s retreat toward the cave mouth, he matched her hurried progress.

Rounding the large boulder hiding the cave’s mouth, he whispered as loud as he dared, “Wait.”

Preoccupied with the nocturnal noises sounding all over the mountainside Melody didn’t heed his warning.

With a desperate lunge, he wrapped his right arm around her and pulled her back, the bags whapping her shoulder. She gave a faint yelp of surprise; turning fearful eyes toward her brother’s face, scant inches from her own.

"Geez. What did you go and do that for?"

"Shhh!" Silurian admonished, louder than she had been. "You want to let the whole mountain know we're here?"

"No, but—"

He cut her off. "It's too late now."

He laid the two sacks upon the dew-covered grass at their feet and inched forward to peer into the dark hole leading into the mountain. He couldn't see a thing. He stood still, listening for unusual noises, sniffing at the air as he did so. Deathly silence and the smell of damp, musty air were the only things to greet his senses.

Another howl split the night air. Closer than the last one.

With wide eyes riveted upon the surrounding mountainside, he bent to the ground, hands fumbling through the grass to locate the two food sacks by feel. Realizing his attempts were futile, he stole a glance at the ground and retrieved them. Holding the unlit torch like a club, he cautiously stepped into the cave's black void.

Melody clutched at his shoulders, causing him considerable pain. She followed him so closely she ended up stepping on his heels more than once. When he stopped just inside the cave, hugging the near wall, she practically pushed him over.

Craning her neck, she whispered in his ear, her lips brushing his lobe, her voice almost inaudible, "Is he here?"

Annoyed at her interruption, he merely shrugged, trying to sense the presence of a creature within the cave.

"Maybe we should light the torch?" Her voice came louder.

Silurian grunted. Nerves on end, he faced her. "Maybe we should just jump up and down and shout, 'Oh Mr. Troll, we're home.'"

Melody let her arms drop to her sides.

Silurian reached into his tunic and withdrew a little piece of flint stone and his knife. A series of blinding flashes jumped from the stone onto the torch in rapid succession until it caught, flaring up and rendering them sightless.

It took him a few moments to reorient himself with this particular cave. It was the original cave they had sheltered in almost a month ago. They had camped within its safety for three nights before their first encounter with Hairy, the troll.

Larger than a country kitchen, the cave consisted of walls and floor worn smooth by centuries of spring runoff. The walls funneled into a crevice at the rear of the cave, leading deeper into the mountain.

He eyed the fissure that served as an entrance to the byways the trolls employed to traverse the catacombs and subterranean vaults of Mount Cinder. "Come on, let's find a nice hard place to lie down for the night."

Melody tried not to smile, but couldn't help herself. He always made her laugh. In spite of everything they went through, he always found a way to put a smile on her face. She guessed that's how he kept going. She followed him to a spot halfway along the wall, equal distance from the night creatures prowling the mountain's exterior, and the trolls and other unspeakable creatures skulking within. The distance itself seemed insignificant should a creature happen to wander into the cave, but it served well enough to keep them hidden from anything casually roaming by the cave mouth, or the crevice. The outside creatures wanted nothing to do with those dwelling within the caves, while the warren denizens were equally wary of those living outside.

"I'm cold," Melody said through chattering teeth as she sat upon the granite floor. The fissures leading into the earth's core served to heat some of the caves they had camped within, but this wasn't one of them.

Silurian positioned himself near the wall, making sure he could see the area around the cleft. He patted the space between himself and the cave wall. "Come here."

She snuggled in with her back to him in an effort to preserve body heat. They lay there for some time, absorbed in their thoughts, Melody quietly sobbing like she did every night. Silurian patted her shoulder, 'shh-ing,' every so often.

Behind them the torch sputtered and went out. Silurian felt her body shiver harder. He gave her a stronger embrace. By and by, she drifted off, her sobs replaced by shallower breathing.

Sleep didn't come as quickly for Silurian. What a day! Uncomfortable and shivering, he idly fingered his knife hilt. Its six-inch blade, sheathed within its cracked and dry, leather case, did little to ease his nerves. Every night was the same. Remain awake into the wee hours of the morning; listening, smelling, sensing.

Of Trolls and Evil Things

The cry of a seagull caused Silurian to scramble onto his haunches. Locating his errant knife, still in its sheath, he fumbled desperately to expose the blade as his eyes stole about the dimly lit cave, probing the darkness around the fissure. Nothing moved.

The steely grayness of the morning sky, visible above the entrance boulder, displayed wispy clouds floating by. A cool breeze wafted into the cave, stirring the tall grass at the base of the boulder. He sighed with relief.

Melody still lay sprawled upon the granite floor, her face pressed against the rock wall. He bent lower to inspect a thumb-sized spider probing the opening in her neckline. Nonchalantly brushing it from her, he watched it scurry away. Walking to the cave mouth, the cooler air raised gooseflesh on his exposed skin.

The mountainside glistened in early morning dew. Birds of all sorts winged back and forth, soaring amongst the heights and the lofty pines clinging to the rock faces. Visible to the side of the boulder, seagulls squawked their displeasure at smaller birds daring to hop too close to their hard-fought scavenging.

He inhaled deeply, taking in the beautiful autumn morn. Hugging himself, he felt a fresh round of goosebumps shiver up his arms. He turned in time to see Melody stir.

She stretched her arms away from the wall, blinked a couple of times and searched for him. She smiled when she saw his silhouette framed in the morning light.

"Good morning, sleepy head."

Watching her lumber toward him, he studied her with concern, until he realized the lines and discolouration on her face were a result of her sleeping against the rock wall.

"Nice face ya got."

She frowned, touching her cheek.

He traced a line curving this way and that, from her temple to below the fat part of her cheek. "I've heard of women putting silly things on their faces before. Mud, crushed fruits and such, but you are the first one, I think, to use a cave."

Melody rolled her eyes, brushing his hand aside. She walked into the sunshine, spreading her arms, welcoming its scant warmth. After finding a place to relieve herself, she returned to the cave.

Silurian crouched in front of the boulder, tending a modest fire within a ring of stones.

She strode past him, walked around the rock, and ventured into the dimly lit cave to retrieve the provision bags the prince had given them.

The cave had a stale smell to it—almost rotten. She hesitated. Trolls loathed sunlight. There was enough light in the cave now that she didn't have to worry, but she scanned the fissure for signs of movement anyway.

Don't be daft, she thought.

She walked to where they had slept and scratched her head. She was sure they had left the two sacks of food against the wall. They weren't there now. Maybe Silurian had them.

She bent down to feel around in the darkness clinging to the walls. Nothing. Her eyes shot to the fissure, barely perceptible at the back of the cave. Swallowing the sudden apprehension gripping her, she straightened, and backed slowly toward the exit, her gaze darting about, but always returning to the fissure.

Smelling the fetid odour grow stronger, her blood went cold.

The telltale scraping of the troll's claws behind her caused Melody to freeze. Icy tendrils of fear shot up her spine. Not wanting to believe what her senses told her to be true, she glanced over her shoulder at the large silhouette of what could only be a troll coming straight for her.

She screamed. Her high-pitched wail reverberated within the cave, echoing many times beyond the fissure. She pitched sideways, scrambling toward the only place she could. The crevice.

The troll growled in delight.

Pausing at the cleft, afraid of what lay beyond the inky darkness, she dared to look back. As if out of a nightmare, another form scrambled toward her from behind the troll. This one on fire!

The cave spun about her, seeming to lurch beneath her feet. The rock floor flew up. A white light flashed in her head as she impacted with the granite floor.

"Nooo!" Silurian bellowed entering the cave, a burning stick in each fist. Unsure what he should do, he threw one at the troll.

The fiery brand bounced harmlessly off the beast's clumped fur and clattered upon the rock floor, coming to rest near Melody's motionless body, but the act had served its purpose. It had taken the troll's attention away from her.

The troll spun to face him. Its yellow eyes squinted, widely spaced above a festering burn it had suffered to its left cheek a few days ago. Snarling, it threw its forearms over its eyes to ward off the hurtful glare of the sunlight permeating the cave mouth, accompanied by the burning light of the torch.

Silurian took the opportunity to drive the second brand into its heaving chest.

The branch crumbled upon impact, not strong enough to penetrate the creature's leathery hide, but more than hot enough to sear its naked flesh.

The troll roared in agony, shooting out its arms in a frenzied attempt to knock it away.

The stick flew from Silurian's grasp. He ducked away from the troll's lunging paws, avoiding its raking claws. He fumbled for his knife. He knew the troll would be fighting its abhorrence of the sunshine filtering into the cave. He needed to take advantage of it if he were to have any chance of making it to Melody.

Hairy roared, throwing its paws back and forth, searching for its attacker. It knew by scent these were the creatures it tracked. The creatures that had caused it pain. Hatred drove it into a frenzy.

A glint of steel flashed in front of it as the bite of a knife opened a large gash along its right forearm.

It shrieked, more in rage than pain. Again, it felt the knife's sting. To its ribs this time, its hard bones deflecting the brunt of the thrust. With a savage backhand, it knocked Silurian away long enough for it to escape into the fathomless darkness beyond the fissure, pausing briefly to scoop up a couple of sacks hidden near the cleft as it stepped past Melody's body.

Silurian scrambled to retrieve the second brand sputtering upon the floor. He waved it side to side to fan the sputtering flame. Holding it in the air before him, he stepped into the gap, his adrenaline fighting to vent itself. He wanted to finish this.

The faint light offered by the failing torch illuminated the immediate area in flickering light. The only telltale sign of the troll, other than the quickly receding scraping of its claws on stone, and its pervading stench, was a low, pained growl.

He turned to face the cave again, hands on his knees, gasping, trying to calm himself. The throbbing sensation in his temples lessened. His hands trembled as he struggled to hold on to the shaking brand.

Melody!

Dropping the torch, he reached her in a single bound. Fumbling along her neckline he tried to locate her pulse, something his father had taught him to do on the farm. He wasn't practiced in the procedure, and before he could find the right location to place his fingers, she rolled her head toward him.

Her body tightened into a spasm. She threw her hands up to ward him off, kicking out as hard as she could. She missed hitting him, but her loud scream pained his ears

"Mel!" Silurian pleaded, trying to make himself heard over her shrieking. He stood up and stepped backward to avoid her thrashing. "It's me."

Recognizing her brother's voice, her screams fell away. She got to her knees, covered her face with her hands, and cried.

He dropped to his knees, and pulled her against him.

She embraced him hard. Burying her face into his neck, she wept.

She couldn't bring herself to relinquish her hold on him. In all the world, his embrace was the only thing that offered her sanctuary. He was her refuge. Her bastion in a heartless, ruthless world. He had put himself in harm's way to protect her. Again. She hugged him tighter.

"It's okay, Mel. It's okay," Silurian soothed, returning her squeeze. He let her go with one arm, easing out of her embrace, and helped her to her feet. "Come on. We need to get out of here." He led her from the cave's dark confines. Slowly. Caringly.

They squinted in the direct sunlight, as they stepped around the boulder fronting the cave. Silurian's fire lay scattered about the ground due to his hasty collection of the brands he used against the troll.

He studied his sister's face. Other than bleary eyes and the beginning of a bruise welling up next to her right temple, she appeared no worse for wear. Physically, at least. He could only hope she wasn't mentally scarred any further than the events of their recent lives had inflicted upon her. He couldn't shake the image of her collapsing before the troll's outstretched arms. He thought he had lost her. He shivered.

Clutching her hands, he turned her to face him so he could inspect her neck. "Did the troll hurt you? I saw you fall..." He almost began to cry himself. "I saw the troll reach for you. You went down in a heap. I, I thought I was too late," he finished quietly, sounding apologetic.

She stared into his peculiar, ice blue eyes, his concern for her blatantly evident. "No, I'm fine. My head hurts a little, I guess. I must have fainted when…" She trailed off, grabbing Silurian's chin in her cupped hands and turned his head to examine his left cheek. "Wow, he sure got you good."

He winced as she probed his cheekbone.

"Doesn't that hurt?"

"Nah," Silurian lied, pulling away. "It'll be alright."

She put her hands on her hips, giving her best motherly impersonation, "You mark my words. If you keep playing with that shaggy friend of yours, sooner or later, you're going to regret it."

He caressed his aching face. "I think I'm regretting it already."

He bent to retrieve the scattered twigs and smoking branches, tossing them back into the fire circle. He was about to ask her to fetch their food, but changed his mind. He began to walk around the rock, but her voice stopped him.

"Where are you going?"

"To get the food," he said, and began to walk again. "Don't worry. I'm thinking Hairy won't be bothering us anymore today."

"They're gone."

Her words took a moment to sink in. He had rounded the boulder out of sight. He popped his head back into view. "Who's gone?"

"Not who, silly. What. The food. The troll, Hairy, must've nicked it."

Silurian disappeared from view. Shortly, he came back around the boulder, throwing his arms in the air. "Great. Now what?"

The Unknown Sea rippled with white caps way off to their left as they picked their way around rock falls and stands of towering pines. Any time now the sun would breast Mount Gloom, the peak named for its penchant of keeping Cliff Face bathed in shadow until midday, but anyone living near the nefarious peak knew better. Mount Gloom derived its name from the notorious events that were rumoured to happen upon its slopes.

A slight breeze blew off the heights, playing with the siblings' hair. Lazy clouds scudded across the sky. There was promise in the air of a warm day; a pleasant respite to the cool, wet weather they endured recently. They walked steadily for a while, putting distance between themselves and the cave, each lost in their own thoughts over their most recent encounter with Hairy.

As they walked, Melody foraged the plants required to make another poultice for Silurian's infected shoulder. They stopped while she prepared the salve and applied it to his shoulder blade. The wound appeared worse than before, but he insisted it was fine. She studied the faint welt on his left cheek, satisfied it wasn't as bad as she first thought.

Silurian inspected Melody's right temple, causing her to wince when he touched the purple abrasion above her eye. Content she was okay, they set off again.

Silurian couldn't help experimenting with his swollen left cheek as they walked. He grimaced every time he puffed it out and sucked it back in again. He repeated this senseless procedure over and over, wondering each time he did it whether or not the bruise was getting better or getting worse. Sometimes he thought one way, sometimes the other.

Tiring of his self-induced medical examinations he studied his sister's troubled countenance.

"I've been doing a lot of thinking about Hairy."

Melody waited for him to continue. When it became apparent he wasn't going to, she urged, "And?"

Silurian stopped walking. "Everything I've ever been told about trolls always included the fact that they detest daylight. Any kind of light, really, but daylight especially. It's said that entire raiding parties of the beasts have broken off an obvious victory come the dawn. Every troll fears sunlight, except our sweet, ol' Hairy."

Mel shrugged indifference. "Ya, it certainly didn't seem to bother him this morning."

"But that's just it. It did!" Silurian responded, gesturing with his arms as he spoke. "The light bothered it to distraction. Yet, it sat in ambush in our cave for who knows how long, while the morning sun filtered in."

Melody watched a pair of seagulls fight over a scrap of fish one of them had dropped on a nearby promontory. "It couldn't have been too long. We're still alive. It must have snuck into the cave after I woke up."

"Ya, you're probably right." He grew quiet for a few moments before adding, "I think we've pressed our luck with Hairy long enough."

He watched the seagulls. The smaller one snatched the scrap from the larger one's beak, jumped into the air, and wheeled out of sight. Squawking mad, the larger gull gave chase. Silurian smiled.

"I've been thinking about what you said yesterday. About staying in Cliff Face."

Melody's eyes lit up, a smile cleaving her dirty face.

"Although I don't like the idea of having to brave the street life after dark, I'm beginning to think we would be better staying within the city where help is possibly nearby. I still think a cave is safer, but Hairy has me troubled. If he's becoming bold enough to venture into the early morning light, who knows how long it will take him to get over his fear of daylight altogether. When that happens, we'll really be in trouble."

The warring birds fluttered in the distance far below, spiraling out over the frothy waters.

His voice dropped to a whisper, "I guess we could always find a cave on Mount Gloom."

Melody shivered. She gulped, taking in his profile. He was watching their seagull friends winging away, disappearing from view behind the bulk of Mount Cinder's shoulder, only to reappear again, farther away.

He couldn't be serious? Could he? She wouldn't go without a fight. She had been told many ghastly tales concerning that gloomy peak. She spent many hours in her mother's embrace as a result.

The sun had dropped behind Mount Cinder's summit by the time they reached the knoll above Redfire Path, basking the valley of Cliff Face in cool shadows.

Melody stuffed her hair into her tunic as best she could. She turned without having to be told, allowing Silurian to neaten the job. He patted her shoulder when he finished.

Few people travelling Redfire noticed them scramble down the steep bluff to join the ambling horde making its way to and from the city gate. Enough people travelled the roadway to allow them inconspicuous passage beneath the barbican and into the throng bustling along the dusty, main artery leading into the heart of Cliff Face.

An unusual buzz stirred the crowd today. Muffled mutterings of treachery and murder. Silurian couldn't help eavesdropping on the idle conversations as they made their way along the busier than usual street toward the market. He caught snatches of words like: big man—scarred face—four skilled fighters—five or six bodies lying in a large pool of blood—Fatal Damsel.

Fatal Damsel? The words echoed through his mind, trying to find relevance. Images from the previous morning assaulted him. The uneasy feelings he experienced crept back to him. The big stranger dogging them through the alleyways. The four men stumbling out from underneath a faded sign with the flaking inscription, *The Fatal Damsel*!

Nah. It couldn't be.

Pure coincidence.

He grabbed Melody by the front of her tunic, practically yanking her off her feet, and pulled her into a doorway.

“What?” she said with alarm. Seeing the fear in his eyes, she grabbed the front of his tunic when he didn’t answer.

His mind was elsewhere, scanning the masses, searching for something in the shadows.

She shook him harder than she meant to, the gesture bringing his attention back to her.

“Sil. What is it? What’s wrong?”

He released her tunic, shook off her grip, and continuously scanned the street. When his eyes found hers, it was if a demon had taken up residence behind his mad stare.

She didn’t think she could have broken eye contact with him had she wanted to. So enrapt was she, his harsh whisper, when it came, almost caused her to scream.

“Do you remember seeing that man in the shadows yesterday?” He kept glancing around, looking for something.

“The guy with the poor mule?” she scoffed. “Of course, but—”

He grabbed her tunic, pulling her face against his, causing her to stumble into him. “No. Not the merchant,” he said through gritted teeth.

Noting the odd expressions passersby were giving them, Silurian struggled to get a hold of himself, but still held her firm. With a quick glance over Melody’s shoulder, he continued, “No. Not the merchant. Didn’t you see the large man in the alleys?”

Melody stood on her toes, trying to maintain her balance. She placed her hands on his chest to create space between them.

He loosened his grip, but didn’t release her.

“Prince Malcolm’s man? The one who kicked you?”

“No, no, no. Not the knight. They weren’t in the alleys! Geez, Mel, think.” He pulled her closer, his eyes darting every which way. “You didn’t see him, did you?”

“Who? I don’t know—”

“In the alleys. Yesterday. During the storm. There was a large man watching us. Every time I saw him, he would back out of sight.” He scanned the crowd. “The first time I saw him, I didn’t think much of it. But outside that noisy bar, *The Fatal Damsel*, when those men came outside, I saw him again.”

"So."

"So?" Silurian almost shouted. "Haven't you heard the murmuring in the crowd? Doesn't everyone seem, uh, I don't know…edgy?"

Melody pushed aside a loose strand of hair from her eyes. "Yeah, I guess so." She unconsciously reached behind her head, checking her hidden tresses.

"Well, think on it," Silurian said with the haughty arrogance of a grown up. "The large man the townsfolk are talking about, killed four merchant rangers. They say he did it so fast, and so brutally, he must have been a demon." To emphasize the last word, he added, "Not human."

Melody's nonplussed demeanour angered him.

"You don't get it, do you?"

She shrugged, looking at the ground, ashamed of her ignorance, but unsure of what she should be ashamed of. "I can see what that man, or beast, did was awful. How could I not? I don't see what it has to do with us, though. Like, I mean, sure I don't want to meet up with him or anything."

"That's the point." Silurian was vehement. He scanned the street, conscious of the people staring at them. He toned down his excitement. "That man. The one responsible for killing the merchant rangers. He was hunting us." *Or, more specifically, you,* he thought. He didn't want to scare her any more than he needed to.

Melody frowned, "You don't know that. Did you even get a good look at him?"

"No, but something tells me I'm not mistaken. I don't know why he killed those others, but I do know he was stalking us."

Melody put her hands on her hips, cocking her head to one side. "You're imagining things. Hairy's getting on your nerves. You're jumping at shadows. I'm nervous too. Probably more than you are…"

"Mel?"

"…but we can't keep jumping to conclusions every time we hear…"

"Mel."

"…someone's gone berserk and started killing people just because—"

"Mel!" Silurian grabbed her by the tunic again, giving her a shake. "I know it sounds silly, but yesterday morning, when I first saw the man in the alley, I knew he was up to no good. The second time I saw him, and both times I only saw his silhouette, I knew he was the same man, and I know he meant us harm. There's something strangely familiar about him."

She knew by his half-crazed expression he believed every word he said. She wanted to say something to ease his worry, but she only managed a weak grunt.

He scanned the busy thoroughfare for the hundredth time. "We have to get out of the city."

He stepped into the street. When Melody didn't react quickly enough, he shouted, "Now!"

Melody self-consciously scanned the people in the street, seeing all the quizzical faces gawking at them. She stepped beside him, whispering in his ear, "Sil, you're causing a scene. Even if nobody was watching us before, they are now."

Silurian followed her gaze. It seemed like everyone was staring at them. "Come on, I can feel him watching us. We. Have. To. Go. Now."

Melody laughed halfheartedly, "Heh, heh. Um, there are a lot of people watching us."

Silurian grabbed her by the arm, pulling her toward the gate.

"You're hurting me," Melody cried out, stumbling in his wake, struggling to break his grip.

The crowd around them paused to witness the spectacle. They parted, allowing the two bruised and battered teenagers to make their way toward the gate. Murmurs of disapproval about Silurian's treatment of Melody followed them, but no one bothered to intervene.

He released her arm and led the way through the gawking bystanders.

Approaching the barbican proper, he stopped dead in his tracks.

Melody couldn't help but to run into him, pushing him forward another step. Seeing the bone-chilling fear in his eyes, she followed his gaze.

Standing at ease on the far side of the guard hut, arms folded across his massive chest, stood a large man. His one eye stared right at her, his other eye hidden behind a black leather patch.

The colour drained from her face, her jaw hanging open in disbelief. When his sadistic sneer lifted the scar on his left cheek, causing it to disappear beneath the eye patch, she almost fainted.

She tried to scream. No sound left her mouth. She covered the lower part of her face with both hands, her wide eyes searching for the best way to flee.

"I knew it!" Silurian said, grabbing her by the elbow and pulling her after him, deeper into the city. This time she offered no objection.

Jostling their way up the road, Silurian hazarded a glance behind them.

The man was gone.

Hunter Hunted

Cowering in the same alley they had hid in the morning before, Melody and Silurian shook with fear. They pressed their backs tight against the wall of a cobbler's mercantile, seemingly trying to dissipate into the weathered boards digging into their shoulder blades.

"Where is he?" Melody squeaked between panting breaths. "Do you think it was him? Do you really think he was waiting for us? Do you think he's searching for us now? Do you—"

Silurian stepped in front of her, and gripped her by the shoulders. "Get a hold of yourself. Yes, it's him. You believe me now?"

She nodded.

He leaned toward the busy street trying to spot their stalker near the gatehouse, muttering to himself, "It won't be too hard for him to find us with all your squawking."

He stole a quick glance at the throng milling about in the street. He released her. "I don't know what to do. If we stay in Cliff Face he is going to catch us, but maybe we can find help first. If we leave the city, we'll have a better chance of losing ourselves on Mount Cinder, but if he finds us there, we are lost."

"Why don't we go to the baron? He'll help us. Surely he will."

He sighed. Throwing themselves on the mercy of the good baron's charity went against his young, headstrong principles. His father had ingrained those traits into him quite nicely. With his sister's welfare at issue, however, he decided that swallowing his pride to save her life would be a small price to pay.

"Okay," he agreed.

The sun was dropping behind Mount Cinder's lofty heights. "We'd best get a move on. Cliff Face will be in shadow soon. I'd like to be inside the baron's walls before dark."

Melody offered him a faint smile, but her mind was out amid the busy thoroughfare. She couldn't help thinking that the back of every large man belonged to their stalker. That he would turn and stare in their direction, his single eye finding their hiding place. She gulped, "Let's go."

Silurian motioned for her to turn around and started pulling the hair from her tunic and fluffing it up.

She tried to pull away, but he tugged on her tresses, making her keep the back of her head to him.

"What are you doing?"

"Perhaps seeing you with long hair will give him pause. Throw him off enough to give us time to escape."

Her eyes grew wide. She spun to face him, despite his attempt to hold her still. "You see him?"

"No, but I can sense him. He's lurking around here somewhere." He grabbed her wrist. "Let's just hope he's not watching us now, or my little trick will be for naught."

They were about to bolt down the alley when a figure entered its far end and started toward them.

Their hearts skipped a beat.

The man couldn't have gotten that far already.

Not willing to chance it, Silurian pulled his sister into the throng.

They were immediately accosted by ill-tempered people begrudging them the small amount of space they required to move about. The milling horde travelled every which way at once. Making matters worse, every large man around appeared to be looking their way.

Progress was slow. Silurian wondered if they were making any headway at all. He glanced forward to a large, pristine building fronting the street, coming up on their left. A fancy sign hung over its recessed entryway shading two large, well-polished oaken doors, reading: *Quiescent Inn*. He couldn't pronounce the first word, let alone know what it meant. By that standard alone, he guessed it to be a posh resting place. The clean-cut doorman in red, silken livery with golden tassels upon exaggerated shoulders, and gold piping running the length of his pants, only served to punctuate the point.

Silurian's attention returned to the crowd around him. A large hand gripped his right shoulder, painfully spinning him about. With wild eyes, he turned to see a stubble-faced man glaring at him.

"Why don't ye watch where yer going?" the man admonished, waggling a sausage-like finger in his face. "Ya nearly bumped me wagon. An' with me wife unner it, fixin' da axle."

Instead of being afraid, Silurian smiled at the stranger and apologized.

The man held the rear end of a fully laden wagon aloft with one, tree-sized arm, while he steered the lumbering crowd around him with the other. Sweat beaded on the man's forehead, dripping profusely from his hairy nose, but his breathing wasn't laboured in the least.

Silurian found himself in awe, jealous of the farmer's strength. If only.

"Come on, Sil." Mel dragged him from under the farmer's nose. "You're causing a jam up."

Silurian scanned the immediate vicinity. Irate people scowled at him for slowing the pace of the crush even further. He shuffled after his sister, the press of the crowd so close, his nose brushed the back of her liberated tresses.

Silurian couldn't believe how busy the streets were. He mused whether the king himself had come to Cliff Face today. That would certainly attract the hordes from villages along the base of the mountain.

Lifting his head higher, he located the cause of the unusual congestion. A circle of bystanders stood around watching a majestic figure talk to a small group of people. Beside them, a farmer sat irately upon the side of an overturned wagon, his spilled produce being trampled underfoot by uncaring passersby. The resulting bottleneck caused the people to funnel their way around the commotion.

The prince! Silurian recognized Malcolm's golden locks. Everything was going to be alright. He let his body be pushed this way and that by the milling crowd as they inched toward the mishap ahead.

Casually he gazed sideways. They were passing the *Quiescent Inn.*

His blood ran cold.

Standing nonchalantly where the doorman dressed in red silk had been, was the man with the eye patch. Massive forearms folded across his chest, he surveyed the juggling masses nearest him with disinterest. He offered Silurian an ugly sneer, the top of his facial scar disappearing beneath the patch.

There was something about the man that was very familiar. Silurian knew he had met him before, but he couldn't place where. He had been accosted by many foul brutes over the last month.

"What the heck are you…?" Melody began to ask. Her brother had stopped walking. She followed his gaze toward a large building on their left. Gazing quite happily in their direction was the grizzled countenance of the man who pursued them.

She gasped, but her attention was drawn back to their immediate surroundings. The crowd had grown tired of their lollygagging and pushed them out of the way into the crowd heading out of the city.

Someone unceremoniously thrust Silurian into his sister and they both stumbled. He lost eye contact with their assailant. The last thing they needed right now was to be knocked to the ground and trampled.

"Hey!" Silurian protested.

As if in response, a merchant's wagon careened into his back.

"Ow! Watch where you're going mister!"

"Perhaps it'll teach ya young ones to mind where yer going!" a wiry, old farmer shot back, prodding his mule through the press.

Melody bumped into him hard, knocked off balance by the people heading in the opposite direction. They were being jockeyed toward the gatehouse. Away from the prince.

Throwing caution to the wind, Silurian threw his own weight around, as insignificant as it was, in an attempt to regain the centre of the street. He clutched Melody's wrist with an iron grip. If they became separated now, she was lost. They made a little progress into the middle of the street, but they were hard put to avert their backward progress.

With a final thrust, met by countless curses and near misses from out flung backhanders, Silurian pulled Melody into the traffic plodding into the city. Instead of being satisfied to be back amongst the current of people entering the city, he stopped short. Coming toward them, in the middle of the street, was the man with the eye patch.

"Oh, no," Silurian muttered.

Melody didn't have to ask. She located the demented smile between the heads of the people in front of her. Before she could say anything, Silurian nearly pulled her arm from its socket, yanking her into the throng making their way to the gates.

They pushed and shoved their way toward the portcullis, oblivious to the irate curses thrown their way, frantic to escape the menace of the man behind the patch.

Silurian marvelled at how much distance the large man was able to make up on them. It seemed a leisurely stroll through the woods for the man, his mere presence enough to part the crowd.

The blood coursing through Silurian's body had his injured cheek and shoulder throbbing. His limbs became sorer by the moment, bumping and pushing their way, ever so slowly, through the unforgiving masses.

He couldn't help wondering where he had seen the man before. Surely it had been recently. There was something very odd about him. As they approached the gatehouse it started to dawn on him where they might have crossed paths.

A guard watched their approach as they fell under the barbican's shadow. The muscular sentry stepped away from his hut at the portcullis' base at the same time a wagon entered the city, cutting off his advance. The guard cursed the man at the wagon's helm as it stalled before him. He could only watch as Melody and Silurian squeezed their way around the wagon's far side. He demanded they halt at once, but they paid him no mind.

Free of the gatehouse, they scrambled as fast as their legs would carry them away from the city.

The guard, about to turn his unspent ire upon the wagon rider, noticed a large man wearing an eye patch enter the barbican's confines. He wondered how the large man thought he was going to leave the city. The traffic had ground to a halt as the wagon's stubborn mule refused to move.

As if in answer, the large man simply bounded up beside the disgruntled driver. Ignoring the merchant's curses, he stepped easily onto the bench seat beside him, hopped into the open wagon and proceeded to tromp through the payload of lettuce and rhubarb. He jumped off the rear end of the wagon without so much as a sideways glance.

Even had the guard wanted to take issue with the large man, the angry people pushing and shouting all around him prevented him from doing so. Leaning his pike against the massive, rusted chain links shooting up the full height of the open portcullis, he sighed and started toward the wagon's driver, all the while wondering where he had seen the man with the patch before.

They had been in such a hurry to escape the confines of the city that they ran right past the trail leading onto Mount Cinder. By the time they realized their error, there was no way they were going to risk going back.

Rounding the first real bend along Redfire Path, Silurian halted their flight. He bent over and placed his hands upon his knees trying to recover his breath.

Melody jogged up behind him, panting, but in her delirious state she couldn't stop herself from pacing. Walking about in circles, hands on hips and head held high, she attempted to calm herself while keeping a wary eye in the direction of the barbican, unseen around the bend.

Between deep breaths, she wiped her sweaty brow and asked with an air of optimism belying her anxiety, “Do you think we lost him?”

Silurian didn’t want to think about the ramifications if they hadn’t. It boded well they hadn’t noticed anyone resembling the large man come around the bend, yet. If the man still gave chase, he should have appeared by now.

Silurian focused on his sister. The day’s grime and sweat had smeared her soft features. The bruise on her right temple seemed to be losing its colour, which was good. She kept looking up the road toward Cliff Face.

He knew they shouldn’t tempt fate. If the man had been delayed at the gatehouse, they were doing him a big favour lingering along the side of Redfire Path in plain view.

“Come on, let’s get off the road. We need to find a safe place to stay for the night. If Patch is still after us, he’ll have fun trying to find us on the mountain.”

Melody attempted to control her rapid breathing. Rubbing at a stitch in her side with a palm heel, she forced herself to take her eyes off the road. She offered him a halfhearted smile, not excited about having to move again so soon.

Silurian straightened up and put his arm around Melody’s shoulder. He steered her away from the roadway, toward the steep embankment leading onto the heights of Mount Cinder.

They had never entered the mountainside from this point. The initial climb was treacherous, but they soon found an animal trail, thirty feet higher, skirting the roadway. With any luck, it would lead them back to the stand of pines above the gatehouse.

The animal track, hidden beneath a layer of pine needles, wasn’t well suited for human travel. It slithered its way beneath clusters of low hanging pine boughs and around outcroppings of granite that reduced the trail’s width to the point where they had to scooch on their backsides to avoid sliding down the steep slope.

Making their way on hands and knees, they passed the bend in Redfire Path; Mount Cinder’s slope turned with it.

Melody emerged from beneath a mass of dense pine boughs snagging at her hair. She endeavoured to stand, but Silurian dragged her back to the ground.

"What the—?"

"Quiet."

Melody followed his gaze through the trees toward where they believed their usual entry onto Redfire rested. All she saw were more trees.

"What is it? The troll?"

Silurian remained silent, listening to the woods around them. The occasional creak of a wagon trundling along the path reached their ears, but nothing else stirred. His uncanny intuition had caused him to miss a breath, alerting him to an unrealized danger directly ahead. He had no idea what that threat might be.

"What's the matter? I don't see anything."

"I don't either," he whispered, causing her to frown. "Something awaits us. Up on the bluff."

"How can you tell? Can you smell Hairy?"

He remained silent, his concentration elsewhere. He slowly crawled back under the copse of pines.

Melody didn't require any prompting to follow his lead.

Out of sight of possible watching eyes, Silurian turned onto his side. There was worry written all over Melody's face. He could tell she was trying hard not to cry.

He patted her hand. "I'm not sure what it is. Don't ask me how I know there's anything at all, I just do."

He closed his eyes for a moment. Could the troll have overcome its phobia of daylight altogether? Or was it something else?

"Something awaits us up there, of that I am sure."

Melody stared toward the trees in question, silently admonishing herself for being so foolish. If she couldn't see the danger ahead when they had been in the open, how could she expect to see anything now? She crawled backward another foot.

They lay hidden beneath the large pine for a while, trying to control their breathing.

Silurian disturbed the encroaching stillness by pulling at his collar and reaching behind his back in a vain attempt to scratch at an annoying itch beneath the sloppy poultice. Try as he might, he couldn't quite reach it. With a grunt, he latched onto the poultice and yanked. It wasn't a great idea. The sudden jerk tore away the new scar tissue. It was all he could do not to cry out in agony and give away their location when the poultice ripped free. He lost his purchase on the gooey patch and it flew behind him into the undergrowth. They both winced at the noise it made.

Despite her alarm, perhaps fueled by her stress, Melody giggled, "I bet that hurt."

His eyes glossed over. Between clenched teeth he managed to say through the pain, "Wasn't one of my better ideas."

"No, probably not." She faked a grin. "So, now what?"

It took a while for the searing pain to subside to a bearable level. Wiping the tears from his eyes he thought about what they should do. He lacked the heart to tell her what he was thinking. How could he? He didn't have the heart to believe it himself.

He rubbed his forehead in consternation for a moment before betraying his misgivings. "We need to find refuge on the other side of Redfire."

His voice was so low, she hoped she hadn't heard him correctly. There was no way he would suggest entering the slopes of Mount Gloom. She would rather take her chances with the troll.

She forced a smile. "You had me going…Heh-heh…" Her sentence lost its steam, seeing the truth in his eyes.

"You can't be serious. You do remember all the tales about that place, don't you? Hairy would be a pleasant distraction compared to what happens over there. You are joking, right?"

She gazed skyward. Judging by the deepening shadows, they had perhaps another hour or so before the trolls came out to prey.

Silurian followed her gaze through the pine boughs. He thought the same thing. Traversing the slopes of Mount Gloom would be dangerous. Dangerous at any time of the day, according to the rumours, but especially after sunset. Unfortunately, if they remained here, their hiding place would soon become a trap.

"I don't like the idea any more than you, but we can't stay here, and we certainly can't go back to Cliff Face."

He paused, staring through the trees at Redfire Path. The traffic was thinning out as darkness drew nigh, the last wagons heading for the city rattled by.

The threat of wandering trolls became direr the lower the sun sank. As a result, any wayward travellers were long out of sight.

Beside them, barely visible through the heather, Mount Cinder rose sheer for almost a hundred feet above the animal trail before sloping inward to higher elevations above.

"There is no way up Mount Cinder close by that I know of, other than the one Hairy is probably guarding." He smiled for her benefit. It was the first time he had put a name to his fear. "We certainly can't remain here. Unless you wish to become his dinner?"

"Uh, I'd rather not, thank you." Her bottom lip trembled. Her eyes darted in every direction, trying to think of a way to avoid spending a night upon Mount Gloom.

Suddenly she sat upright, brushing her scalp painfully on the low boughs. Dry needles raked her forehead, pricking her eyelids. She winced and ducked her head, but an enthusiastic light shone from her eyes.

"I know. We can follow Redfire Path into the valley. We can ask the nearest farmer to take us in."

Silurian grunted. He pointed to the darkening road. "There hasn't been anybody leaving the city for a while now. You know why?"

Melody swallowed, "Yeah, but—"

"But nothing, Mel. The reason there hasn't been anyone leaving Cliff Face recently is because people—full grown men—know what happens if they are caught outside after sunset. Even if we run all the way, which I doubt we could, we wouldn't reach the valley floor in less than an hour."

"I can run fast. I know we can reach the first farm before Hairy's friends come out. I bet we could…"

"Mel?"

"…be at the first farm in time…"

"Mel."

"…to set the supper table…"

"Mel!"

She stopped her headlong rush. Closing her mouth, she stared at her brother, eyes wild and tearing up.

"We would be *on* the supper table."

She couldn't fight back the racking sobs.

Silurian crept over, holding her close with his free arm. "We'll be okay. You'll see."

The large man smirked. The top of a fearsome scar disappeared beneath his black leather eye patch. His quarry lay low in the thick brush not far from where he waited.

He had lost them the previous day, much to his chagrin, but after a lengthy search, he discovered where they had given him the slip. He found a discarded poultice behind a stand of pines along the pathway leading up to Mount Cinder's interior.

When he lost them today, he quickly realized they hadn't fled up the mountain trail. After eluding the guard at the gate house, he had run straight up the bluff, following the trail leading into the heights. Before long the trail narrowed, traversing a high cliff that commanded a clear view of the surrounding mountainside. He hadn't been that far behind them. There was no way they could have ventured further up the slopes without being seen. That meant they must have gone to ground.

He had spent a few moments scrutinizing the terrain, searching for flaws in the landscape. If they weren't close by, they may have taken flight down Redfire Path. Even so, he was sure they would try to gain the heights at some point before dusk. They wouldn't be foolish enough to ascend Mount Gloom. They would have to come this way. There wasn't another point of entry onto Mount Cinder for many leagues.

He took up a position behind a large boulder overlooking the stand of trees upon the bluff and waited. A twig snapped toward the bend in Redfire Path, but he couldn't see anything. It must have been an animal. A few minutes later he heard it again.

Whatever was in the undergrowth wasn't getting any closer. Fearing his prey might have found another means to access the slopes, he set out in the direction of the noise. Before long, the slope he trod along came to an abrupt halt, rising and dropping before him at sheer angles. Except for a narrow ledge that disappeared into a heavy growth of pine trees, the snaking path nothing more than an animal trail. Unwilling to lose his quarry, he inched his way along the rock ledge, creeping upon hands and knees and trying to ignore the irritating needles jabbing at him.

He had lusted after these two long enough. He felt like he would burst if he didn't find them. He needed release. Tonight, no matter what came, he meant to sate his hunger. Tonight, the boy would pay for the disfigurement he had caused him. His little sister would be the payment. He could almost…

A furtive movement caught his eye. Below him, at the base of the thirty-foot cliff he perched upon, he watched with delight as his prey poked their heads out from behind the cover of a low pine. They watched the path leading toward Cliff Face for a time, before hesitantly, and then quickly, scampering across the roadway. On the far side of Redfire Path, they were swallowed by the low reaching forest on Mount Gloom.

His sneer lifted the patch from his grizzled cheek. He had them now.

From a vantage point a hundred feet above the animal trail, a pair of yellow eyes watched with curiosity as first, two small forms, and then a few minutes later, a larger one, darted across the human trail. An evil grin parted its maw.

Tonight promised to be a good night.

Mount Gloom

Gnarled, grotesquely twisted trunks, thicker than Silurian's arm span, choked the waning light from the world; the darkening sky unseen beyond a canopy of intertwining branches, hundreds of feet above the spongy, forest floor. Mist rose from the humus, casting the mountainside in an ethereal pall. Outcroppings of shelf rock were darkened blurs in the fog, interrupting the rolling slope of forest floor which was cloven by fissures that dropped away to depths unknown. Accompanied by the cold air and dampness, and smelling of rot, Mount Gloom's atmosphere lived up to its name.

The first fissure they encountered marring the forest floor, almost proved to be their last. Silurian noticed it in the nick of time and jumped the narrow cleft, but Melody pulled up short. Her left foot slipped in the thick leaf carpet and hovered precariously over the gap. She flailed her arms frantically, regaining enough balance to pull back.

Seeing she was safe, Silurian put his hands on his knees to catch his breath; each laboured pant evidenced by the steam leaving his mouth in cadenced puffs. He straightened out as Melody caught up, but she dropped unceremoniously to her rump. Flopping her arms across her lap, she stared at the dead foliage before her, her chest heaving.

Silurian listened for signs of pursuit, or any other sound they both feared might be following them. He shivered. The cold forest dampness raised gooseflesh on his exposed, sweaty forearms. He wanted to tell her to get up. They needed to keep moving if they wished to find a place suitable to spend the night, but he knew she needed to rest.

Hands on his hips, he arched his back, slowly stepping in a tight circle, taking in the entire forest. Which direction should they travel? Ascending the slope would lead them into lower temperatures. Without shelter, that would be an issue. To descend the…

His breath caught in his throat. Twigs snapped in the direction they had just come.

Melody heard it, too. She jumped to her feet, staring that way, but she couldn't see anything through the mist.

Just when they thought perhaps it was their imaginations running wild on them, the sound of brush being trampled underfoot reached their ears. Much closer this time.

A branch broke somewhere beyond the mist.

They gasped, looked quickly at one another, and bolted in the opposite direction. Away from Redfire Path.

Silurian ran as fast as his sister could manage. Someone, or something, crashed through the woods behind them, hard on their heels, its form not quite visible through the mist shrouded foliage. They could tell by the sound of its passing, it was large.

To her credit, Melody kept pace. Twice in as many minutes, they were forced to slow their frantic flight and find their way around a gaping fissure. Skirting the edge of the second crevice, Silurian wondered what fate awaited anyone unlucky enough to drop into one of those abysmal holes and survive. He didn't care to imagine what kind of nightmarish creatures might be lurking within the depths, awaiting anyone unlucky enough to fall their way.

Beyond the fissure, they were about to continue their headlong dash, when the mist cleared before them. The route they travelled ended at the brink of a wide chasm. They scrambled to a stop a few feet from the lip of a nasty defile scarring Mount Gloom's northern exposure, the gorge bottom lost in heavy mist.

Melody gave her brother a ‘now what’ look. She was tired, hungry and scared. She knew he was too.

Before he could respond, a bloodcurdling scream reached them. It was all they could do to keep from jumping over the edge. The sound of a vicious scuffle ensued.

Shoulder to shoulder, foreheads nearly touching, they craned their necks in an effort to locate the combatants. They stood frozen with fear.

A second howl, deeper and fiercer than the first, got their feet moving.

Silurian stepped back toward the last fissure they had rounded. Toward the mournful cries.

Melody frowned. “Where are you going?”

“Someone needs our help.” He peered over his shoulder, but she wasn’t following. “If we help them, perhaps they’ll help us.”

“Are you crazy? How do you know who, or what, is fighting back there? You *want* to become its next victim?”

“You don’t know that. What if…”

“Sil?”

“…it is someone just like us…”

“Sil.”

“…who is in desperate—”

“Sil!”

“What?” Silurian snapped, but he couldn’t help keeping the slow smile from spreading across his face. She had just handled him the way he always dealt with her whenever she rambled on without making sense.

“Think about it. Who in their right mind walks the slopes of Mount Gloom. Especially at night?” She threw her hands in the air and let them drop to her sides, muttering, “Besides us, of course.”

He stopped walking, unsure what to do. Another howl, similar to the second one they heard, but oddly different, caused his skin to crawl. There was a sense of finality in the tone.

The forest fell silent. Whoever, or whatever, had been fighting back there was finished. It was only a matter of time before they became its next target.

Silurian reversed his course. Making a beeline for Melody, he pulled her after him, recklessly picking his way down the edge of the defile. They needed to get away from here fast. He didn't know how easy it would be to climb into the higher reaches of Mount Gloom, but he reasoned the temperature would at least be warmer at lower elevations, so down they went, mindful of the ominous crater yawning on their right.

Scree and loose rock slid away beneath their hurried footfalls, the slope so steep in places they were forced to slide for stretches upon their backsides, hoping their momentum wouldn't take them sideways over the lip of the crevice. In a couple of places, they were forced to turn and scale down the face of a granite ledge.

More than once they almost slid off the edge of a small cliff. Some of those drops were only twenty feet or so, but the debris of jagged rock and broken timber at the bottom of these defiles would surely prove fatal were they to fall into it.

Every so often a loose pebble or two would follow them down from the heights above, the debris not necessarily the result of their own passage. The ever-darkening wood abutting the edge of the abyss assisted their descent, providing them with much needed handholds.

Lost in the gloomy twilit mist, the dull roar of the Unknown Sea venting its fury upon Mount Gloom's granite shoulder, pounded far below as the last vestiges of waning sunlight glinted upon its distant, steely waves.

Silurian spotted a hollow in the face of a twenty-foot drop, several feet above a pile of rubble. With a little luck, the suspicious depression would lead them to a cave. He made his way to the edge of the rockslide and slipped and slid down the accumulation of broken granite, nearly twisting a knee in his haste.

Reaching the bottom, he surveyed the naked rock face. The depression was indeed the entrance to a cave. It was fronted by a cabin-sized boulder, its sloping sides affording him a way up. To his left, the mountainside disappeared into a fathomless, shrouded abyss. From the corner of his eye, his sister skidded her way down the rock fall. She fell to her bottom and careened along the loose rocks with a series of grunts and squeaks until she 'harrumphed' against the jumble of broken stone at the base of the scar.

Silurian scrambled up the large boulder, its far edge separated from the cave's lip by a four-foot gap. He peered into the fissure. The depression extended into the mountain further than the twilight allowed him to see. It ran into the mountain and veered to the right. It would have to do.

He started to urge Melody to hurry up, when a shower of pebbles cascaded over the lip of the ledge above the cave mouth, pelting him. He covered his head with both arms until the falling debris subsided.

Fearing the worst, he wasn't prepared for the sight snarling down at him.

A seven-foot troll stood atop the cliff face, glowering. Its massive chest, marred by a recent burn, heaved. Beady eyes filled with menace glared at him above yellowed, chipped teeth. The festering gash upon its forearm removed any doubt about its identity. The waning daylight didn't seem to be bothering Hairy at all.

A long trailer of spittle dangled from its mouth, stretched, and fell. Silurian sidestepped the drool as it smacked the boulder.

Not taking his eyes from the feral beast, for fear that Hairy would leap at them from the brink, he motioned to Melody. "Hurry up. Hairy's come to pay us a visit and he doesn't look very happy."

Melody hadn't needed the coaxing. Her voice beside him caused him to jump, "I'm not too happy about it myself."

She shivered, though she wasn't cold; the sheen of perspiration on her face proof of their panicked flight. Above her loomed black death. Below her, the mountain dropped away into a fathomless mist. Before her, a darkened hole marred the face of Mount Gloom, leading to unknown depths. The prospect of what they might encounter in the pitch darkness beyond the cave scared her almost as much as what watched them now.

Not taking her eyes from the panting creature, she asked, "You think it's a good idea to go in there?"

Silurian swallowed. He was wondering the same thing. Once in the cave, they would be blind. Hairy, on the other hand, would see better. He fumbled inside the folds of his tunic, fingering his knife handle. He was about to say as much, when his sister suddenly screamed.

The troll dropped right down into their midst, a terrifying howl escaping its gaping maw; huge paws extended, razor-sharp claws spread wide.

They sidestepped quickly, trying not to fall from the boulder to the jagged rubble below.

Fully outstretched, the troll slammed onto the rock surface with a sickening thud. Its breath left its lungs upon impact—its howl truncated by the sudden stop.

Silurian withdrew his knife, prepared to pounce, but stopped short when Melody screamed again.

Her trembling hand indicated the hilt of a curved knife protruding from Hairy's back.

An evil laugh sounded from the ledge the troll had just vacated.

Silurian tried to swallow the fear threatening to choke him. Without having to look, he knew who was up there. He desperately wished he was wrong.

Melody shrieked, covering her mouth with her hands.

Silurian slowly raised his head, now realizing who the two combatants in the mist had been.

The grizzled man gazed upon them with a satisfied sneer, his ugly facial scar snaking its way beneath his black eye patch. A thin stream of blood ran down the side of his face.

Silurian stumbled, dropping to his knees to avoid falling off the boulder. Images flashed through his mind about his last encounter with this brute.

"Aye, that's right boy. It's me."

Silurian swallowed hard.

"What's he talking about?"

Silurian couldn't find his voice.

The large man answered for him, "Tell the little lady, *Si-lur-i-an*."

The way the man said his name, dragging out each syllable with a mocking lilt, was unnerving.

"Tell her how ya put yer nose into business nae concerning ye."

The man spat, barely missing Silurian's shoulder, smacking the boulder beside the troll's body.

"Tell the little darling there how ya stood up for that wee thieving bitch. How ya saved 'er punishment at me hands by lying yer fool head off."

He spat again.

"Tell her!"

This time the spittle impacted Silurian's cheek with a wet smack. Silurian winced at the feeling, his nose wrinkling at the smell. He wiped off what he could with his hand and rubbed his cheek on his collar.

Melody remembered Silurian's tale from the marketplace. It was the time he had first met Prince Malcolm. "We have to get out of here. He's going to kill us."

The man chuckled and began descending the slope.

Silurian tensed. Gazing at the chunks of broken rock at the base of the boulder, he knew the man would reach it before they could. With no other way up the face of exposed rock, the only route left to them was the cave.

At least it wasn't the troll chasing them. The darkness should prove advantageous if they could make their way into the depths of the mountain.

Stepping around the troll, they leapt from the large boulder into the noticeably cooler temperature of the cave. Outside the crunching of stones underfoot and their assailant's audible curses as he slid into the granite debris around the boulder, marked his approach.

Just as Silurian expected, the cave took a right-hand turn. Bumping their way along the back wall, groping its cool surface, they followed its contours. Soon the cave mouth was no longer visible. They were enshrouded in total darkness.

The harsh, laboured breathing of their hunter grew louder as the man's leather boots scuffed the granite at the cave's entrance.

In front of them, the cave ended.

Thonk

"Oh, no," Silurian muttered more to himself than his sister. He slapped his palms along the cave wall. Up high, down low, fervently trying to locate an escape route. "Oh, no. Oh, no, no, no."

The small side chamber wall they patted down turned back toward the main cave. The absolute darkness hid the terror on their faces as they searched the inky blackness trying to catch a glimpse of the man.

They clasped each other, shaking, their eyes riveted on the space they knew he would come. Listening intently, anticipating his imminent arrival, only the wind and the occasional staccato of a distant seagull's call reached their ears.

Silurian tried to swallow, but couldn't. The knife hilt in his hand did little to ease his rising dread. There was only one way out of the cave and it involved going through the man lurking somewhere in the darkness ahead of them. He felt sure this man was responsible for the brutal slayings in Cliff Face yesterday. He tried to swallow again. He couldn't.

Suddenly the man was there. When it seemed the darkness couldn't become any blacker, the man's presence appeared as a perceptible shadow. Judging by the way the shadow bobbed about, he couldn't see them.

Their breath caught in their throats.

Left with no other choice, Silurian tightened his clammy grip upon his knife and plunged it into the black abyss.

Melody screamed.

Silurian's knife caught nothing but air. He had miscalculated the man's proximity, but his effort was enough to gain their stalker's attention.

The man's consequent lunge elicited another reverberating screech from Melody that resounded throughout the cave with agonizing acuteness.

Silurian grabbed her tunic by the shoulder, the first thing he could locate in the dark, and yanked her after him. His face brushed a sweaty forearm as they squeezed past the man, scrabbling frantically along the wall at the back of the cave.

The man reached out for them, but missed.

The cave mouth came into view, the outside darkness a bright contrast to that within, as moonlight filtered into this section of the cave. Where the man had gotten to, they had no idea.

Seeing the opening, Melody broke free of Silurian's grasp and bolted for freedom.

She ran headlong into the clutches of the one she so desperately sought to avoid as he stepped from the shadows.

The man wrapped a huge forearm around her midsection, lifting her from her wildly kicking legs. With a throaty chuckle, he declared, "Ah, ha. I have ye now, lassie. I have ye—ow!"

Melody's teeth found purchase in his burly forearm.

"Why, ya little slut," he spat, tightening his vice-like grip around her waist.

Air escaped her lungs in a violent rush.

His free hand swung at her face with brutal force.

"I'll teach ye some respect, missy. Ye'll see."

Silurian reached out in a desperate attempt to stop his sister, but missed. He stood against the wall, trying to discern the man's whereabouts. Something in the darkness to his left darted out.

Melody screamed.

A cold sweat washed over him. The brute had his sister.

The man's howling anger, followed by the sound of a loud skin smack, spurred Silurian into action. He thought better of attacking blade first for fear of stabbing Melody.

He ran straight into the man's left shoulder, the impact knocking the brute back a step.

The man grunted with the effort of maintaining his feet while keeping a firm hold on his prize.

Silurian closed on him. Slower this time. His knife poised to strike. Just when he thought he should be able to make contact, a huge fist smashed his nose against his skull, lifting him from his feet. He crashed to the granite floor, several feet away.

The ensuing jolt caused him to lose his grip on the knife, the air leaving his lungs upon impact. His head cracked against the cave's rear wall bringing a halt to his slide. He fought with all he had to remain conscious.

The last thing he heard was the metallic clinking of his knife skidding out of reach.

"Silur—oomph!" Melody tried to call out.

The man released his bear-like grip on her waist and spun her about. Applying a crushing grip on her shoulders he forced her body against him.

With her nose pressed painfully into his chest, she placed her palms against his ribs in a vain attempt to pry herself from his smelly body. Try as she might, she could only turn her face sideways.

"It's time for me reward, missy," he purred.

His breath in such close quarters made her want to retch.

"It's time for me reward."

At fourteen, she knew exactly what he inferred. She fought harder to break free, but her struggles were useless.

Curiously, he rocked her. Pressing his body against hers, his rough hands found their way beneath her worn tunic. He caressed her back.

Tears fell from her cheeks. No one was going to help her this time. She didn't know where Silurian had gotten to. Hopefully he was on his way to Cliff Face to find help. Wherever he had gotten to, the brute didn't seem too concerned. Why would he be? There was no one around for leagues of this cave. The chance of Silurian finding his way back here in the dark was slim. Even if help did come, it wouldn't arrive until well after the deed was done. If she was lucky, she would pass out before the brute had his way, but she feared that wouldn't fit into his plans.

His hands slid around to her sides.

"Please stop," she begged between sobs.

To her amazement the man stopped, his thumbs coming to rest below her small breasts. His evil laughter shattered the silence in the cave.

Melody flinched. Outside, the moon rose above the Unknown Sea, washing the cave in soft light. The man's wicked, broken toothed mien grinned down at her.

If she could find a way to stall him, she might be able to keep him in the cave until help arrived. It would probably be too late for her, but perhaps retribution might be delivered upon her malefactor. Perhaps by prolonging events, she could save some other hapless girl from the misfortune of crossing his path.

He forced her backward. Melody tried to backpedal, but he shot a leg out behind her, tripping her up. His fingers dug painfully into her ribs, arresting her fall and gently easing her to the cold granite floor; she but a leaf in his massive hands.

"I loves it most when they begs, sweetie," he chuckled, kneeling over her, his knees straddling her legs. Clutching her wrists in one huge hand, he held them above her head, steadying himself on the floor with his other. His tongue licked his lips. Spittle waggled off it to smack sickly upon the edge of her lips.

She closed her mouth, fighting the impulse to vomit, and wiped her face as best she could on her shoulder.

He made a move to force his right knee between her tightly closed thighs. “Beg for me, sweetie. Beg for me. The louder ye scream, the more ye’ll enjoy it, ye’ll see.” His rapturous laughter resounded hollowly within the cave.

She couldn’t believe this was happening. In her wildest nightmares, she never once imagined her life ending this way. Silurian warned her what could happen if she were caught unawares upon the streets of Cliff Face after dark, but his words had in no way prepared her for the stark reality of the emotions coursing through her now. The terror. The fear. The humiliation. The shame.

Silurian had been right all along. He had put up with her complaints, her crying, her moody behaviour toward him, to protect her from just such a fate.

Tears streamed down her cheeks. She wished he was here now. She needed to apologize to him. She needed to tell him she understood why he refused to live in the streets. Why he risked his life, forever moving from cave to cave, cold and hungry, battling the troll. He had been doing his best to spare her from just such an outcome.

Most of all, she needed to tell him how much she loved him.

The man’s efforts brought her mind back to the present. She shook her head back and forth wildly, as if the act would prevent the man from achieving his goal. And then his knee was between her legs. She gasped at the relevance.

In his struggles, he had let her right hand slip from his grasp. She slapped his stunned face harder than she thought possible. The impact stung her hand with such intensity she thought surely her hand had been set afire.

“Why you little bitch.” He spat a mouthful of foul saliva into her face and punched the side of her head so hard the blow left her on the brink of unconsciousness.

Grabbing the collar of her tunic with both hands, he tore it open, ripping it clean to her waist. He roughly snatched it out from underneath her, practically tearing her left arm from its socket as he did so. To his chagrin, she wore a simple shift beneath her tunic. He reached up to—

"Leave! Her! Alone!"

Silurian left his feet, impelling his body weight into the man's left shoulder, reaching out to clutch the man about the face. His fingernails scratched the man's rough complexion.

The man grunted with the impact. Silurian lost his breath. The momentum of the collision drove the two from Melody's semi-conscious body as they crashed to the floor in a heap of rolling arms and legs.

The man's fists flew about in a wild rage, striking nothing but air more often than not, but a few blows managed to glance off various parts of Silurian's body.

Silurian grappled the best he could, concentrating more on avoiding the man's swings than delivering his own. Only his blind rage prevented him from being instantly overpowered, but the momentary advantage of his surprise attack waned quickly. In the soft moonlight, it was all he could do to avoid the clenched fists of fury coming his way.

Melody sat bolt upright. Her heart skipped a beat. Her breath caught in her throat. Terrified and groggy, she had trouble recalling why. The sounds of a scuffle reached her in the darkness.

Trying to clear her blurry vision, she squinted and wiped the tears from her eyes. She was in a cave. It spun slowly about her. Shaking her head, she concentrated. Two silhouettes jostled near the cave mouth, one much larger than the other. The smaller one fending off blow after blow.

Silurian?

Her eyes focused. *Oh, my Lord! Why are you still here? That means help isn't on the way. Oh Silurian, what have you done?*

"Sil?" she called frantically. "You need to get out of here! You have to get help!"

Silurian paused for the briefest of moments at the sound of her voice. A fist caught him squarely in the left eye.

Silurian grunted. He fell away from the man, seemingly ever so slowly. The sounds in the cave became muted. A high-pitched voice tried to reach him, but all he could make out was an incoherent buzz.

The cave floor loomed up to greet him. White light flashed within his skull as his head impacted the granite.

"Sil!" Melody screamed. She tried getting to her feet, but as soon as she gained her knees, vertigo grabbed her, whirling the surreal atmosphere in the cave in all directions at once. She collapsed to her chest. Shaking her head, she tried again. Reaching her knees, the cave spun. She refused to let herself fall. If she didn't move now, they were both lost. Getting to her feet, however, was going to be another matter entirely.

The large man bent over her brother's motionless body.

"Get up," she sobbed. "He's going to kill you!"

The large man grabbed Silurian by an elbow and ankle, his huge hands having no trouble grasping the boy's slight limbs. Standing straight, he hefted the limp form like a sack of oats and stepped toward the cave mouth.

Melody's eyes grew wide. She shook her head in protest. "No," she implored, choking on her terror. "Don't hurt him. Please, please, don't. Please, no."

The large man smiled at the half-naked girl crawling wretchedly toward him. He winked. "Aye lassie. I knew ye would beg." He gave her a self-satisfied smirk and turned to face the cave mouth. "They always do," he chuckled. "They always do."

"And now for ye," the large man spoke to Silurian's unconscious form. "Ye have been a nettle in me hide fer more 'n ye can know. It's cause o' ye, good ol' Thonk lost his eye. Snitching me out to the prince in the marketplace like ye did. He done give me a choice. Me hand or me eye. Ye an' that miserable street whelp ye saved from the farmer are t' blame for good ol' Thonk's dilemma. If ya hadda kept yer snotty nose outta me business, I wouldna be forced to come after ya."

He craned his neck to see his prize struggling to reach him, crying hysterically and reaching out with flailing hands. She fell to her face more often than not. A throaty laugh escaped him. It was going to be a good night.

"Nooo!" Melody cried out, watching in horror as the evil thing who called himself Thonk, swung Silurian's body behind him.

Without a pause, he reversed the direction of the swing and flung the boy from the cave.

Melody could do nothing but watch. Her brother's body flew through the air, disappearing out of sight toward the jagged shards of broken rock below. Almost at once she heard the unmistakable sound of his muffled impact.

She fell wailing to the floor, covering her head. She had just witnessed her brother's demise. The only person left to her in the entire world. The one person who wouldn't think twice about dying to save her, had done just that. Except, he hadn't saved her.

Thonk turned to his reward. How he lusted after this one. Now she was his. Life was good. When he finished with her, he would pick up the trail of that little wench who attacked him at the farmer's stand. He had been closing in on her a few days ago, when he had first spotted Silurian and this girl enter the alley during the rainstorm. He recognized Silurian as the one responsible for his run in with Prince Malcolm, and now he had dealt with the boy, just like everyone else who crossed good ol' Thonk. Of those there had been many. In fact, he had dispatched four decent fighters outside *The Fatal Damsel* that same day. He smiled at the memory. No one got the better of Thonk and lived to brag about it. Prince Malcolm's turn was coming. He would make sure of that. But first, his prize.

The girl lay on her stomach holding her head in her hands, wracking sobs swelling her lithe form beneath her semi-transparent shift; soiled and wet with sweat.

He smiled. She was ready.

He bent at the knees and said in a mocking, tender voice, "There, there, little one."

Grabbing her by the shoulders, he turned her over and pulled her hands from her face.

All the will had been sapped from her. She lay submissively, awaiting her fate.

"No need to cry. Thonk's here for ya. Ain't nobody here but us now, dearie. A special night for ye, eh?"

Drool slid down his chin in anticipation. Absently, he swiped at it with the cuff of his filthy tunic, unclasping his sword belt as he did so. The belt fell with a metallic clatter to the floor.

Eagerly fumbling with the drawstrings of his breeches, he succeeded in knotting them in his haste. Instead of cursing his misfortune, however, he relished the delay, taking in the sight beneath him. Awaiting him. Wanting him.

He attempted to pull his pants over his hips, but they were bound too tight. Tongue between his lips, he concentrated on undoing the drawstring in the semi-darkness. The task proved difficult, but no matter. They had all night. He turned to the cave mouth, utilizing the moonlight. Finding the right string to tug, he started to pull on it when his light disappeared.

"What the?" was all Thonk managed to spit out before a huge, hairy paw raked his face, sending drool, scraps of flesh and tendrils of blood flying across the cave mouth.

A bellowing roar reverberated within the cave.

Thonk heard the girl scream behind him as the force of the blow lifted him from his feet and sent him sprawling dangerously close to the cave's lip.

The man forgotten already, nostrils flaring, the troll started for Melody.

She got to her knees, but fell screaming to her back. She crab-walked into the dark, away from the feral beast everyone had left for dead.

She couldn't help thinking through her terror, what an ironic twist of fate. A short while ago, the man who called himself Thonk, had come to their rescue by supposedly slaying the troll upon the cliff, and now the troll had saved her from Thonk.

She hit her head against the cave's back wall. A surreal sense of calm overcame her. What did it matter? Troll or man? Either way, she died tonight. She could only wonder, why? What had she ever done to harm anyone? And Silurian? Her brother was a saint through and through.

Scuttling along the edge of the wall, her foot slipped on something loose, scraping the granite as her foot passed over it. It was too dark to see this far back in the cave. She reached out to discover Silurian's knife.

Perhaps she had a chance after all. She wrapped her fingers around the hilt and rose unsteadily to her feet. With any luck, one good swipe with the blade as she ran past and she just might avoid Hairy's gangly arms.

Hairy advanced methodically, its eyes tracking its prey in the dark with acute precision. It tilted its head to one side, seeing the creature it stalked alter her path. She had risen from the ground and held one of those fearsome metal fangs those creatures used when they attacked its brood.

Hairy watched the frail creature, with hair only upon her head, dart to the left in an attempt to get around. Hairy howled at the sport, sidestepping into the little creature's path, who in turn lashed out with its artificial fang.

Hairy stepped back to evade the lunge, the brief pause enough to give the little creature the advantage she needed.

Melody darted for the cave mouth, coming to a sudden stop at its edge, trying to locate the large rock in the soft moonlight. The boulder lay off to her right.

Her slight hesitation proved her undoing. As she tried to leap out, a hairy arm grabbed her from behind, spinning her about to face the very nightmare they had been eluding for over a month.

She gazed into the beast's bloodshot, yellow eyes. The troll's snout seeped a disgusting fluid, and an awful stench of rotting meat emanated from its breath. Large, chipped, yellow fangs dripped slobber onto a festering wound upon its chest. She tried to shrink down, but the weight of its heavy paws held her firmly.

It lifted its head to the moon to howl in triumph.

A metallic scrape was the only warning either of them had before a whirlwind of death leapt from the cave floor with sword in hand. Lucky for Melody, she stood much shorter than the troll. The whistling sword took the beast's head clean from its shoulders.

Melody screamed. Hot gore sloshed over her. She tried to disengage herself from the lifeless body, but its claws still held her shoulders fast. Its falling, dead weight, threatened to topple her out over the lip of the cave along with it. Fighting to remove herself from its grip as it tumbled sideways, she caught a glimpse of the jagged rocks beckoning to them from below.

"Oh no ye don't, lassie," Thonk managed to sputter through the half of his face that wasn't shredded.

Grabbing her left arm in his massive hand, he snatched her from the troll's clutches as Hairy's body teetered on the brink of the cave mouth. Thonk urged the carcass over the precipice with his boot, to follow its recently departed head.

As the troll spun away, Melody could see the knife Thonk had previously used in an attempt to dispatch Hairy atop the cliff, still firmly embedded in its back. Together they watched it somersault down the face of the drop, coming to a sudden, spine-snapping stop on the jagged rock debris below.

Distracted by the course of events, it dawned on Melody who held her now. She stomped on his foot to break his grasp.

Thonk yelped in surprise, but his iron grip held her fast. He grabbed her other shoulder with the hand clutching his sword and spun her to face him.

She gasped at the sight of what remained of the right side of his face. Thonk's right cheek had been shredded by the troll's massive paw. It hung in loose scraps of skin, dangling grotesquely below his eye patch. Melody could see his back teeth, red and bloody, through the hanging strips of gory flesh. She turned her head away, spitting up.

Thonk shook her violently, causing her head to snap back and forth with such ferocity that she thought for sure he would break her neck.

"Look at me, little witch. Look at me! This is all your fault. Look at what that brute of yours has done to good ol' Thonk's face. If ya hadn't struggled so much," he lisped, his words slurring due to the damage done to his face. Blood splattered her face as he half spoke, half spit.

Even had she wanted to, with him shaking her so hard, there was no way she could focus on him.

He shoved her across the cave mouth. It was all she could do to stop herself from pitching headfirst over the brink. She landed heavily on her back, an arm and leg dangling in thin air. She rolled into the cave, trying to regain her feet—her back to him. Before she could straighten up, he thrust his boot against her raised butt and shoved her face first into the cave's side wall. Her nose and teeth took the full brunt of the impact.

She quickly flipped into a sitting position, fretting over the crazy man's advance. Blood trickled from her nose and her tongue toyed with the sharp edges of broken teeth. She spat out the gritty shards in a thick gob of blood. All the while, her fearful eyes never left the deranged man brandishing his sword above her.

The undamaged corner of his mouth turned up, "Aye, witch. Jus' ye an' me now. Ain't nobody to bothers us anymore, me thinks, eh? Tis time to reap me bounty."

Thonk flourished his bloody sword tip scant inches from her face before dropping it to her midsection and lifting the bottom of her shift. The razor edge left a trail of blood where it touched her skin.

Her eyes grew wide. She wanted to push the sword away, but touching the fiendish weapon would surely sever her delicate fingers. Trembling, she tried to force herself through the solid granite wall behind her as the sword's edge sliced its way toward her chest.

A cascade of pebbles and small rocks showered down from above the cave outside. Thonk rolled his eyes at the interruption. Were they ever going to leave him in peace? He withdrew his blade, cursing his rotten luck, "What now?"

A man's voice sounded from outside the cave, "Hello? Is anyone down there?"

Thonk stiffened. He recognized the voice. *Now what?* If they found him here like this, it wouldn't go well. He whirled on Melody, practically putting his sword into her mouth, preventing her from making a noise. "Quiet, wench, or I'll slice yer tongue from yer head. Ya git me?"

Melody gave him the slightest of nods, her eyes crossing as they watched the blade wavering a whisper's breadth from her face.

Thonk turned his attention to the man outside. *I wonder how many are with him?* With the slightest voice he could muster, he slurred, "Help me. I'm in the cave. I'm hurt. Oh, please hurry."

Melody started to shuffle sideways, but one look from Thonk stopped her short. Tears streamed down her face, mingling with the blood dripping beneath her trembling lower lip. Eyes wide, she watched the brute squeeze up against the inside of the cave entrance; slipping into the shadows, but still close enough to dispatch her should he choose.

From outside they heard the man scramble down the steep slope. They could tell by the wavering light outside, he carried a torch. His footfalls crunched to a halt at the bottom of the slide.

The newcomer's sizzling torch and his laboured breathing reached their ears as they listened to him mumble something to himself in a tone of wonderment. They couldn't make out what he said, but it sounded like he was inspecting the broken carcass of the troll.

Thonk worried the man would see Silurian's body amongst the rubble as well.

"Oh please, hurry. I'm hurt bad," he said in his best, whiny girl's voice, blood spraying as he talked. Had he been able to, he would have smiled at his own resourcefulness as he listened to the man's hurried climb, boots scrabbling for purchase as he gained the boulder.

Melody stared. Her eyes grew wider than before.

Prince Malcolm stood upon the boulder, squinting into the cave. His sword was sheathed within a baldric upon his back, the jeweled hilt sparkling in the moonlight over his left shoulder. Melody shook her head in tight little jerks, eyeing Thonk in case he was watching her feeble attempt to warn the prince.

Oh, please no. She thought. *Not the prince too.*

The prince's scrutiny of the dark cave came to a sudden stop when he laid eyes on the girl's frail little body, covered in dark stains, most likely blood. Her head twitched, probably from the fright she had suffered at the hands of the troll. *Poor little thing.* Noticing all the blood on the cave's floor, he wondered how such a wee thing could have beheaded a troll. He could tell she was hurt. He bent his knees and hopped into the cave's darker interior.

The girl screamed.

The prince smiled, thinking he startled her.

From the corner of his vision, the moonlight glinted off something metallic.

Instinct alone saved him.

Without thinking, he ducked. A sword whistled by above him. The swing's momentum so powerful it carried the sword and its wielder into an unbalanced spin, punctuated by a jarring clang as the weapon struck the cave wall. The sword shattered upon impact in a flurry of sparks and clinking steel shards that fell away along with a fist-sized chunk of granite.

Malcolm reached over his shoulder, grasping his sword hilt with amazing speed.

Thonk's battering ram fist was faster.

Melody screamed.

Oh, no. No, no, no, no. Not again. Now the brute would kill another person. A prince, no less.

The punch's force lifted Malcolm from his feet. He landed hard, his head cracking upon the granite floor. He knew he had to keep his wits about him. He was dead if he didn't.

He hoisted himself up with his elbows, but Thonk launched his huge frame through the air, landing with devastating force, straddling his chest. Malcolm's head rebounded off the floor, addling him further.

Thonk reached into the inside of his right boot and withdrew a nasty, curved blade. He spun it effortlessly in the air, adjusting his grip so he could thrust it into his prone victim. He stopped the swing in midair, his other hand holding the stunned prince by the throat.

"Ah, what a night it has been. First the boy, then the troll, an' now ye. An' I ain't even got to me dessert yet." His ensuing laugh left no doubt he had gone completely mad. Blood dripped from his gory face in an erratic stream, dripping into the prince's blinking eyes.

The knife wavered. Thonk added with a contemptuous slant to his voice, "Tis time for ye t' die. Say hi to yer brother for me. I'm sure he'll remember fondly the last person he saw in this world."

Thonk lifted his head high, laughing maniacally. He gripped the knife hilt tighter and cried out.

Melody screamed, cupping her mouth with her hands, cowering sideways, away from the confrontation.

A third voice joined the cacophony.

"Why don't you say hi to him yourself, you son of a bitch!" Silurian shouted, driving the knife he had extracted from the troll's back, one of Thonk's very own curved blades, deep into the grizzled man's neck, the deadly weapon severing Thonk's windpipe. Silurian didn't stop thrusting until the guard came to rest against Thonk's right shoulder.

Thonk's eyes bulged from their sockets in agony and disbelief. His upraised hand released its grip upon the curved knife he had meant to dispatch the prince with. It dropped to the ground, clattering and bouncing slightly. His hands grasped at his mortal wound.

Silurian moved to the inside of the cave, and with a mighty shove, pushed the huge man off the prince and out over the brink.

"And say hi to Hairy while you're at it," Silurian spat as he watched the man's body cartwheel down the slide. A faint gasp of breath escaped Thonk's neck wound as his body broke upon the jagged rocks below.

Silurian staggered to his sister's side. He slid down beside her, his right shoulder hammering into the cave wall, stopping him with a jolt, but he cared not. He grabbed Melody's blood-covered body and pulled her into his embrace.

She tipped toward him, but didn't return the hug. Stiff with fear and utter exhaustion, all she could do was tremble and weep.

Silurian wiped at the blood drooling from her mouth with an edge of his threadbare tunic, all the while stroking her head softly, whispering, "There, there. It's all right. It's over now. Everything's going to be just fine. I've got you."

Daydreaming About a Nightmare

Seagulls squawked overhead, frolicking in the air currents swirling about the high battlements that encircled the white towers of Castle Svelte; the spires a stark relief against a pale blue sky.

Ring Lake's waves broke against the rocks along the eastern ramparts, hundreds of feet below. The lake's surface churned under the same stiff breeze snapping the colourful pennants fluttering above the multitude of spires crowning the royal seat of Zephyr.

Fields surrounded the three land-locked sides of the walled city, teeming with wildflowers and shrubbery, awash in early spring sunshine.

It had been a long, hard winter, more severe than anyone could recall, but the snow was all but forgotten, the countryside painted in various shades of green. Upon the plains, furry creatures scampered about, stopping every so often to sniff at the air. Evidenced by shimmering puddles dotting low lying areas, rain had fallen overnight. Colossal shadows meandered across the gently rolling land, following great puffs of white clouds drifting overhead.

Standing several hundred feet above the city, three figures enjoyed the vista from a vantage point high upon the keep's tallest spire. They rested their elbows contentedly upon the crenellated balcony wall encircling the midst of the wizard's tower. Even from the tower's mid-section, they stood higher than all the other peaks shooting up from the massive rooftop of Castle Svelte.

Silurian craned his neck to see the underside of a higher balcony, another hundred feet above them. That balcony belonged to the resident wizard and nobody, except perhaps the king, was allowed up there without the wizard's consent.

The tower, aside from its loftiness, wasn't any more remarkable than any other part of the castle, but its very nature gave it an eerie persona. Many locals crossed themselves whenever they caught themselves gazing at the Wizard's Spike.

Silurian smiled. He should attempt another foray up the forbidding inner stairway and sneak his way to the top sometime soon.

He and his sister had lived in the royal palace for almost half a year now, and yet, looking at all the flamboyance and pomp that castle living offered them, he felt certain that at any moment he would wake up and find himself lying upon a cold, dank, rock floor, fearing for his sister and running from Hairy. Their twist of fate seemed incomprehensible, even now. He shook his head. Never in his wildest dreams would he have imagined being part of such grandeur. Not just to see it, but to actually live it.

Prince Malcolm, heir to the Ivory Throne, stood beside him, laughing and pointing at something upon the lake, his flaxen locks buffeted by the wind.

Melody stood on the other side of the prince, squinting her eyes to follow his outstretched arm.

The prince's injuries, as a result of their encounter with Thonk the previous autumn, had been severe. After catching sight of Thonk in the busy street as he assisted with directing traffic around an upturned cart, he had gathered his men and went after the brute. Earlier in the day, an eye witness had identified Thonk as the one responsible for the multiple murders outside *The Fatal Damsel*.

Malcolm was an accomplished tracker, and once he realized that Thonk had taken to the slopes of Mount Gloom, he had ordered his men to split up in an effort to cage the man in.

When Prince Malcolm had stumbled upon the bizarre scene outside the cave, his wariness of Thonk was thrown off by the sight of the half-dressed, battered girl.

As a result, Thonk had ended up breaking Malcolm's nose and cracking his skull. The prince had lain unconscious, attended only by Melody and Silurian throughout that fateful night. In the wee morning hours, Malcolm's squire, Jarr-nash, had found them. With his help, they managed to get the prince back up the mountain face to where others of the royal guard came across them and rushed them all off to Cliff Face.

Back at the baron's manor, the healers had cleaned up Silurian and Melody as best they could and sent them on their way.

For over a week Malcolm's condition had been touch and go, and then one day, the swelling abated and he regained consciousness.

Silurian remembered well the daylong vigils he and Melody had been part of outside the baron's gates as they lived amongst the mass of concerned, city residents. During those days of prayer, they had had no need of shelter or protection. They were absorbed into the crowd that had gathered and camped at the baron's gate awaiting word of the kingdom's favourite son.

Scraps of discarded food were plentiful. Until the morning they received word that Malcolm was out of danger.

When news broke that the prince would survive, the crowd stood and cheered, praised whatever gods they worshipped, and dispersed. It was time to move on.

Melody and Silurian spent the remainder of that last day wandering the lower marketplace searching for more food scraps or an opportunity to earn such, before setting out for the familiar reaches of Mount Cinder.

Approaching the city gate, destitute and weary, they were recognized and stopped by the same guard who had been on duty the day they had fled from Thonk. The guard immediately escorted them back to the manor where they were greeted by a humble and apologetic baron.

Malcolm, upon regaining consciousness after the eighth day, had immediately dispatched his personal guard to scour the city for the peasant boy who had saved his life. How ironic, Silurian mused. They had been right there all the time.

Silurian remembered well the day the King of Zephyr had come galloping into Cliff Face with a grave look upon his face. The day before Malcolm regained consciousness.

He also reminisced, for at least the hundredth time, about that wondrous day when they were introduced by Malcolm to the very same King of Zephyr in the baron's Great Hall. King Peter Malcolm Svelte, ruler of the mightiest kingdom in the free world, had requested an audience—with *them*!

Silurian had immediately prostrated himself before the king, but was sternly bidden to rise. He almost fainted when he did so, for the king bent his own knee instead, bowing his head in respect and gratitude toward the quaking boy.

"Silurian Mintaka," the king said to him, "I am forever in your debt. Not only have you given me back my son, but more importantly, you have given back to the people of Zephyr, *their* son. Only the gods have the right to take him from this world, therefore, I must surmise you were sent on their behalf. For your bravery, my sword is forevermore yours to beckon," the king's voice dipped to an almost inaudible tone of reverence.

If that wasn't enough, the king had then stood, only long enough to drop to a knee in front of Melody.

"And you, my fair Maiden."

Melody almost fainted.

Silurian grabbed her by the elbow to prevent her from toppling over.

"You have proven yourself as courageous as any of my best men. Zephyr is forever in your debt. Whatever you need, whatever your desire, all you need to do is but ask."

Neither child could speak.

The king rose to his feet. With a curt nod from Prince Malcolm, everybody else in the baron's Great Hall fell to their knees, clasping their right hands to their chests and bowing out of respect for the two waifs that had just recently been begging in the streets in an attempt to survive. The genuflection of the masses was for Melody and Silurian.

The king smiled and wiped a tear from Melody's cheek.

A *king* had wiped *her* face!

The king then cupped their chins in his large hands and lifted them to look him in the eyes. “You need never lower your gaze in my company again. It is I who shall look upon you with awe.” He raised his voice to include the congregation, “I have been informed by Prince Malcolm you have lost your parents.”

They offered timid nods, sensed only by the king who still held their chins upon his regal fingers, his ornate rings a-twinkle in the rush lights. The king smiled even more.

Releasing the two, he addressed the masses, bidding them rise with a gesture from his upturned palms. His deep voice resonated throughout the hall, “I, King Peter Malcolm Svelte, sovereign of Zephyr, Lord of the Ivory Throne and Defender of the Realm, do hereby declare, Silurian Mintaka, son of Zorn Mintaka of Cliff Face, and Melody Mintaka, daughter of Mase Storms End, niece of Lord Therin Storms End, are hereby bestowed the most honourific title, Peers of the Realm.”

A collective gasp escaped the crowd. A Peer of the Realm was a title rarely bestowed upon anyone other than nobility. It hadn’t been awarded in over fifty years. A Peer of the Realm, once named, was considered a member of the royal family in every aspect, but blood.

Prompted by King Peter’s lead, a windowpane rattling ovation shook the Great Hall.

The crowd noticed the king preparing to speak again and the din subsided.

“This morning, Prince Malcolm knighted his previous squire, Jarrnash. He requires a new squire to attend Firerider.”

Firerider was Prince Malcolm’s horse. A horse so fine it was rumoured to have royal blood.

The king gave Silurian a solemn nod. “He has asked for you.”

It was Melody’s turn to grab Silurian’s elbow.

Silurian stood before the king, prince, and all the assembled noblemen and women, abashed; goosebumps rising upon his arms and back.

Melody prodded Silurian in the ribs with an elbow to break him out of his stupor. He sputtered, “I-I would be honoured, my liege.”

He scuffed the toe of his tatty boot upon the polished oak floor board, wanting to add something else, but too intimidated to do so.

The king lowered his voice so only those in the immediate area could listen, “The honour would be mine, young Silurian. I can honestly say, if *I* had to choose a successor for Jarr-nash, and I assure you, he will be hard to replace, I couldn’t have picked someone braver, nor more honourable than you have proven yourself to be.” He paused to gesture at the man standing behind Malcolm’s right shoulder. The same man who had ridden beside the prince when the lead horseman had shoved Silurian into the dirt with his metal boot. The same man who had found them in the dark after the traumatic events in the cave on Mount Gloom.

“Not to worry, young Silurian. I believe I know what’s on your mind.” The king nodded. “Melody shall be given a spacious room in the princess’ wing of Castle Svelte. You will be able to see her at your leisure—”

Prince Malcolm cleared his throat.

The king roared, “When you are not attending your knight, of course.”

Melody jabbed Silurian in the ribs with her elbow, an action she seemed to enjoy doing.

He shook his head, his mind returning to the lower balcony of the Wizard’s Spike. His sister faced him sternly, hands on hips, hair whipping about her face.

“You didn’t see it either, did you?”

Silurian had no idea what she was on about, his mind not fully back in the present. Watching his sister’s mouth berating him, he mused idly that the king’s wizard had done a great job repairing her teeth.

“You weren’t even listening. Were you?”

He raised his eyebrows, turning to Malcolm for help.

The prince balked, backing away a pace, shrugging his shoulders, wanting nothing to do with it.

Melody turned on her green leather, knee-high boots, plopped her elbows on the balcony's thick ledge and grunted in disgust.

"I'm sorry Mel, I was somewhere else."

"Humph. You are always somewhere else." She spun to face him, the abruptness causing Silurian and the prince to jump back a step. She pointed an accusing finger at her brother, wagging it. "I know exactly where you were. You were thinking about Hairy again." She waited but a second before demanding, "Weren't you?"

Silurian couldn't answer quickly enough. His attempt to hold back a smile only served to fuel her consternation.

"You were, weren't you?" Incredulous, she opened the same hand and gestured wildly around. "I knew it. I knew it! Here we are, enjoying the view of the lake, musing about who might be sailing down there—what they're talking about—and, and you end up daydreaming about a nightmare." She turned her head away, disgusted.

She turned back again just as quick. "I don't know about you sometimes, oh brother of mine. I really don't. I think you feel sorry for what happened to that," she shrieked her disgust for the creature, "that beast!" She stared at him for a moment, before glaring at Malcolm, daring him to come to Silurian's defense.

It was all Malcolm could do not to smile.

"Well?" She returned her glower to her brother.

Silurian took a step backward, the corners of his mouth turning up. "If Hairy's unconscious body hadn't broken my fall when Thonk tossed me out of the cave, we wouldn't be having this conversation, would we?" He stepped back again, thinking about how his body must have landed on the troll and then rolled off the boulder where he had lain half-conscious in the darkness, unseen by Hairy or the prince. When Hairy's decapitated body had fallen from the cave a short while later, it had landed near him, with Thonk's knife still in its back.

"But, since you brought it up, I couldn't help thinking our furry friend is probably in a better place."

"Huh? That's absurd. What would make you say something like that?" she demanded, walking forward, keeping pace with him. "Honestly, I worry about you sometimes."

"No reason, really. But, I always wondered how Hairy managed to find us time and time again. I could never understand why he wanted to hurt us so bad. In fact, now that I've thought about it, I'm thinking he never meant to harm us at all."

Melody frowned, stepping forward faster to match her brother's retreat. "What in the *world* would make you think that?"

"Well," he started slowly, taking a moment to wink at Malcolm who walked behind her. "After sleeping in those caves with you for over a month, I think that all poor Hairy was trying to do was stop that awful sound from resonating throughout his underground world."

She stopped, puzzled. It was the silliest thing she had heard him say yet. "Awful sound? What awful sound?"

Inching backward, Silurian retorted, the words coming fast through barely restrained laughter, "Why, your snoring, of course!"

Before she could respond, he spun on his heels, dashed around the balcony to the open door and bolted inside. His fingertips hung up momentarily upon the jamb, giving him that little extra purchase he needed to make the turn without losing pace.

Her jaw dropped. She turned to Malcolm.

Not missing a beat, the prince added, "Why do you think," he declared with as much gravity as he could muster, his voice cracking at the end, "the king gave you the tower bedroom?"

Speechless, all Melody could do was watch as the prince rounded the balcony and ducked through the same doorway.

An echoing cacophony of laughter resounded throughout the tower, following the boys' quick descent of the spiral stairway within.

The End...

...or is it just the beginning?

If you enjoyed this book, please watch for the Epic Fantasy series, *Soul Forge*, a story about a forgotten hero who is shunned by his kingdom, and yet, without him, life as they know it may soon cease to exist.

Please visit my website: www.richardhstephens.com
If you wish to keep up to date on new releases, please subscribe to my newsletter by clicking on the contact tab on my website.

You can also look me up on Facebook:
https://www.facebook.com/RichardHughStephens/

A little about me.

Born in Simcoe, Ontario, in 1965, I began writing circa 1974; a bored child looking for something to while away the long, summertime days. My penchant for reading The Hardy Boys led to an inspiration one sweltering summer afternoon when my best friend and I thought, 'We could write one of those.' And so, I did.

As my reading horizons broadened, so did my writing. Star Wars inspired me to write a 600-page novel about outer space that caught the attention of a special teacher who encouraged me to keep writing.

A trip to a local bookstore saw the proprietor introduce me to Stephen R. Donaldson and Terry Brooks. My writing life was forever changed.

At 17, I left high school to join the working world to support my first son. For the next twenty-two years I worked as a shipper at a local bakery. At the age of 36, I went back to high school to complete my education. After graduating with honours at the age of thirty-nine, I became a member of our local Police Service, and worked for 12 years in the provincial court system.

In early 2017, I resigned from the Police Service to pursue my love of writing full-time. With the help and support of my lovely wife

Caroline and our five children, I have now realized my boyhood dream.

www.ingramcontent.com/pod-product-compliance
Lightning Source LLC
Chambersburg PA
CBHW020614310726
48979CB00008B/1486/J

9781775103653